SUMMER AT WORLD'S END

Summer At World's End is the second book featuring the Fielding children. Again, Tom, Carrie, Em and Michael are fending for themselves and surrounded by lots of animals. Carrie and Lester rescue a beautiful horse and Carrie, in a dangerous rescue bid, is saved by Charlie, the dog. When Charlie's fate is in danger, the children put up a tremendous fight to save him. The Fielding children are never without ideas for making a little money to keep their cheerful home together.

Monica Dickens, the great-grand-daughter of Charles Dickens, lives with her husband and two children in America, surrounded by horses, cats and dogs. *Follyfoot*, her bestseller for children, published in Piccolo, is shortly to be followed by *Dora At Follyfoot*.

The House At World's End, the first book in the World's End series, is also published in Piccolo.

Also available by Monica Dickens in Piccolo

THE HOUSE AT WORLD'S END
FOLLYFOOT

Summer
at World's End

MONICA DICKENS

Cover and text illustrations by Peter Charles

A Piccolo Book

PAN BOOKS LTD
LONDON

First published 1971 by Wm Heinemann Ltd.
This edition published 1972 by Pan Books Ltd,
33 Tothill Street, London, SW1.

ISBN 0 330 02958 4

Made and printed in Great Britain by
Cox & Wyman Ltd, London, Reading and Fakenham

AUTHOR'S NOTE

The lines of poetry quoted in the book are from the following poems:

'Don John of Austria . . .'
  – from *Lepanto* by G. K. Chesterton.

'Blow, bugle, blow . . .'
  – from *The Princess* by Tennyson.

'I hate the dreadful hollow . . .'
  – from *Maud* by Tennyson.

'Birds in the high Hall Garden . . .'
  – from *Maud* by Tennyson.

'And a voice said, "No. Not for Right Royal . . ." '
  – from *Right Royal* by John Masefield.

One

'Quick, Carrie – come quick! There's a horse in my garden!'

Michael's garden was only a small plot behind the hen house where a few carrots and radishes fought a hopeless battle against strong weeds, but Carrie's young brother was furious. His pyjama trousers were drooping, his straw hair on end, his face red with sleep and anger.

'I *dug* that garden. I *sowed* those seeds. *Watered* them. Gave them the best years of my *life*!'

Michael kept thumping the bed to make Carrie open her eyes, but Carrie only said, without opening them or even waking properly out of a dream of moonlight steeplechasing, 'Get the horse out then.'

The gaps in the hedge of the meadow behind the house were patched with old bedsteads and bits of planking and broken hurdles. Carrie's horse, John, or the piebald pony Oliver Twist, or Leonora the donkey, quite often broke out. They wandered over the garden and stuck their heads through windows to see what was going on indoors; but they never went off anywhere.

'It's not one of ours.' Michael pulled down the blanket and found Harry, the smallest puppy, sleeping beside Carrie.

Carrie sat up. Harry sighed and shifted into the warm dent where her shoulder had been. She went to the window. It was a gusty night. The moon swept over the slope of the meadow, chasing the wind. John was standing by the bottom gate, head up, mane and tail blowing like a prairie horse, watching the dark shape that moved in the shadow behind the hen house.

Carrie called to him. John answered softly and swung his

7

head up and down, putting his foot on the bottom bar of the gate to rattle it. The dark shape lifted its head and moved into a patch of moonlight where bits of laundry were drying on the gooseberry bushes.

It was a small chestnut horse, short-backed with a fine head well set on an arched neck.

'They come to you,' Carrie's friend the dairy farmer had told her long ago when they first came to live here. 'If you're a born horse fool, they'll come to you.'

And John had come. Well ... they had stolen him. Snatched him from the jaws of death, to be exact. The donkey had escaped from a cruel junk man, been hit by a car, and brought here, blind in one beautiful eye. Oliver the Welsh pony had come, needing a home. And now this little chestnut horse. Carrie knew everybody's horses round about. This one was a stranger.

'You see,' she said to Michael, 'the word does get round. Animals know they're welcome here.'

'They're not welcome in my vegetable garden.' Michael hitched up his pyjama trousers and Carrie noticed that his feet were muddy.

'Did you try to catch him?'

'He put back his ears and wanted to bite me.'

'Perhaps he wants to stay.'

'I don't want him.'

'Mike – he's a *horse*!'

Carrie put Michael into bed with the puppy, and went down the wide creaking stairs and out through the kitchen. Joey, the black woolly monkey, was sleeping in a chair by the stove, hunched like a little old lady, with his piece of torn blanket over his head. He opened one eye at Carrie, then closed it again, munching his gums.

The path outside was dazzling white. The moon raced into a cloud and out again, travelling the wind. Trees moved and murmured. Bushes were alive with wind. The weeping willow by the pond floated like hair. Carrie's long sand-coloured hair blew round her face. She took it out of her mouth to call to John, 'Who's your friend?'

'What a ghastly shock,' her father sometimes said, 'if one day he answered you.'

'He does.'

Horses could tell you things without speaking. It was only people who had to tie things down with words. It was obvious what the strange horse in the vegetable garden was saying. As Carrie went towards him, he laid back his small ears and backed away, snorting.

'Don't you like the smell of people?' Carrie put her hands behind her back and leaned forward to blow gently down her nose. Most horses would respond to this. Not this one. Perhaps he didn't like Carrie using horses' language. He didn't trust people.

She moved forward. He backed away. Over Michael's radishes. Over the sunflowers that had sprouted from last winter's seed falling out of the bird house on the elm tree.

He watched Carrie. She watched him. A good thing, because he suddenly whipped round and lashed out with his heels. His shoes flashed in the moonlight.

Once there was a famous horse trainer called the Whisperer, who could gentle the wildest rogue horse by whispering into its ear. But Carrie couldn't get anywhere near this horse, much less its ear.

Idea. She went to the shed and took out Lucy, the brown Nubian goat. Lucy loved horses. She stood underneath John to get shade in the summer. In winter, she slept with him in the stable, chewing her cud while he chewed hay. In the vegetable garden, she raised her head with the long silky ears like a girl's hair. The chestnut horse dropped his nose. They discussed. His ears moved back and forth. Perhaps he would follow the goat.

'Come on, Lucy.'

A goat never comes unless you give it a good reason, so Carrie went to the dustbin and took out a soup tin. The glue under the labels was Lucy's favourite snack. Carrie held out the tin. Lucy made a sideways chewing movement of her small prim mouth and came towards her. Carrie let her have a lick, then backed round by the side of the house towards

9

the stable yard, holding out the tin. Lucy followed. The horse, as if he had nothing better to do, moved after her. The wind blew the moon into the clouds, and John galloped away into the dark.

The yard was closed in by buildings and an old brick wall. The front gate to the lane was shut. When Lucy and the horse were in the yard, Carrie dropped the soup tin, shut the side gate and went back to the house. From her window upstairs, in the coming and going of the fitful moon, she watched Lucy poking about, knocking over a bucket, bumping at the door of the feed shed, walking after the soup tin as it rolled away from her tongue. The horse stood still in the middle of the yard, head up, staring into the night.

He was very beautiful. Carrie's fancy set her on his back, jumping the brick wall, the hedge across the road, sailing over the countryside while heads turned to stare at the beautiful horse, and Carrie the only one who could ride him.

In the morning, Lucy had licked the tin shining clean, put her foot through the old chair Michael used for a mounting block, and broken into a sack of potatoes. The chestnut horse was gone.

There was a note on the kitchen table from Tom, who had gone early to work.

'Girl came for horse. Was very rude. To me *and* to horse.'

Two

Tom was Carrie's older brother. He worked for a vet on the other side of the hills, where the beautiful green country was stained with new red brick houses and black streets. Tom wanted to be a vet too, but no one in this family had any money for college, except Uncle Rudolf, and he wasn't going to cough any up.

Carrie's younger sister had been christened Esmeralda, so she called herself Em. Michael was the youngest. He was small for his age, and one leg was shorter than the other, so he walked a bit up and down, as if he were on the side of a hill or the edge of a kerb. He sometimes wrote his name Micheal or Micel or Michale. Why should everyone spell the same? When he read aloud, it was like listening to a new and curious language. Miss McDrane at the school said he was impossible to teach. But it was her sort of teaching that was impossible. Not Michael.

Their father, Jerome Fielding, was a restless seafaring man with very white teeth that grinned through a black beard. He and Em both had thick curly hair that wouldn't lie down. Em used to spend hours trying to flatten hers by wetting it, binding it down, even ironing it. But when her father came home from trying to sail round the world in a home-made boat, and she saw that his hair was like hers, she let her own spring up again in dark wild curls, like his.

He had only got about a quarter of the way round the world. His boat had sunk without trace in the Roaring Forties, so he had come home to get another.

While he was at sea, the children's mother, Alice Fielding, had almost died saving Michael's life in a fire that burned down the old Army hut that was their home. She got Michael out just in time, but a falling timber broke her back. When she went to the hospital, her children had to go and live with rich Uncle Rudolf who had found money in plumbing, but not a kind heart. He didn't want them, and they didn't want to be there. His wife Valentina wore clothes made out of dead animals, and was driven mad by children. And dogs. And cats. Even a hibernating tortoise.

If they had stayed, there would have been murder done. So Uncle Rudolf let them move to his old stone house in the country, empty for years, except for rooks and mice and memories of olden-day voices.

It was falling to bits and a long way from nowhere. It had

11

once been an inn. Wood's End Inn, because it stood on a corner where the road came out of the green tunnel of a tall beech wood. After the fast new road was built on the other side of the hills, no travellers came this way any more, so the village people began to call it World's End Inn.

World's End. It stood in grass, with the hill meadow behind. Thatched stables, cart sheds, a great black barn, weathered to grey, where field animals ran in and out through the broken boards. Grass in the thatch, the wall of the yard crumbling and green with moss and ferns. Everything leaning and dilapidated. Everything perfect.

Tom and Carrie and Em and Michael had cleaned it out and patched it up and lived there free and alone before their mother came out of the hospital and their father rolled in from the sea. Not alone. With animals. At first there was only Charlie – part poodle, part golden retriever, part hearthrug – and the four cats who had made Valentina scream, 'I am going mad!' twenty times a day.

Gradually others had come. Other cats. Other dogs. Chickens. Lucy the goat and a sheep called Henry. A rabbit. A lovebird. The donkey Leonora. Oliver Twist and John. Joey, the black woolly monkey that Carrie had found, sad and shivering, in a pet shop.

Money was always short, but somehow they scraped along. Tom had his job with the vet. Em went out baby-sitting. Carrie's horse John pulled the brown trap to do shopping errands, and also pulled the muck cart to sell manure over at the housing estates. Michael did odd jobs in the village for pennies. Carrie was going to sell her poems one day. Somehow they just managed to feed themselves and all the animals.

Michael counted that there were a hundred and ten legs at World's End.

'If I could have kept that chestnut horse,' Carrie said, 'it would have been a hundred and fourteen.'

'If you could have *stolen* it, you mean.' Her father was sitting with his elbows on the kitchen table and his bare brown sailor's feet on Charlie's rough back, stretching his

12

mouth round a huge sandwich filled with everything he could find in the larder. Joey, the little black monkey, sat on his shoulder and picked crumbs out of his beard.

'Saving a life isn't stealing.' Carrie looked at her friend Lester, who was sitting on the floor with the three puppies, Dog Tom (to be different from Boy Tom), Dick, and Harry. Lester and Carrie had stolen the brown horse John last year, on his way to the slaughterhouse. They didn't wink or grin at each other, or make mystery signs like Em and her friend did to put you outside their secrets. Carrie and Lester looked straight at each other with a blank expression that said everything.

'The chestnut must have been ill-treated.' Carrie sat opposite her father at the big round table that could have fed twelve or fourteen, if they ever had that much food. It was scarred with the initials of everyone who had lived here. Her brother Michael had carved W F, with his first initial upside down. Her father had gouged a deep J F and a triangular sail. 'It's natural to a horse to like people, you know, after living with them for such hundreds of years.'

'There have always been rogues and bad lots.' Her father did not share her life's passion.

'But they didn't breed from those. They bred from the best and gentlest. That's why we can ride them, although they're much stronger than us. They *want* to be told what to do. Years and years ago, you see, when horses ran in herds, they had to follow the stallion leader, for safety, and so—'

Her father put his free hand over his ear, which had a gold ring through it.

'I'm only telling you.' It was surprising that grown-ups did not want to learn. 'I'm only telling you why I know that chestnut horse is in trouble. Lester and I are going to try and track his hoof prints today and find out where he is.'

'You're not, you know.' Her father spoke through the last chunk of bread and tomato and sausage and pickle and cold baked beans and stood up. Joey took a flying dive to the top of the dresser and sat there, picking his teeth with a match. He had to be top monkey. He always had to be higher than

13

Carrie sat opposite her father at the big round table

the tallest person in the room. Once when Carrie's father was up a stepladder hanging a picture, Joey had jumped for the washing-line under the kitchen ceiling, and teetered there like a tightrope walker.

'You'll track no horses today, Carrie. You're coming up to London with me. Your Uncle Rudolf won't lend me any money, so I'm going to try and get a newspaper to buy me a boat.'

'*The Lady Alice*?' Carrie's father already had a blue seaman's jersey with the name of his new boat across the chest, although he hadn't yet got the boat. 'Why should they?'

'So they can print the story I'll write. "Sailor of the Seven Seas." It will make our fortune.' He had been predicting that for as long as anyone could remember. 'College for Tom. Horses for you, Carrie. Thoroughbreds, horses to race—'

'She'd never do that.' Lester got up from the writhing mass of puppies. 'Don't you know that racehorses only race because the jockeys excite them to panic?'

'Nonsense, boy. They love it.'

'Yes,' Lester said darkly. 'Like a fox loves being hunted.'

'Don't look at me. It's not my fault.'

Lester made Carrie's father a bit nervous. He was a quick, extraordinary boy with a pointed goblin face and a fore-lock of hair over dark, bright eyes. He did things that no one else did, or would believe, if they were grown-ups. He knew things that no one else knew, like where the birds went when it snowed, and what it felt like to be an elephant, and what happened to you after you were dead. Very surprising. Very extraordinary.

When Carrie was with him, she sometimes felt that she went downstairs without touching the steps. He came with them to London, and in the Underground Carrie got separated by the crowd and thought she flew down the escalator between the framed advertisements.

Three

They went to the offices of the *Daily Amazer* on the bank of the River Thames, a tall glass building which flashed back the sun to the beautiful day. Carrie's father was so sure that everything was going to go beautifully, to match the day, that he put off going into the office and took Carrie and Lester for a boat trip on the river.

They ate their sandwiches and threw the crusts to the gulls that had come screaming upriver from the sea. A man began to play a mouth-organ, so Lester took his mouth-organ out of his pocket and joined in. They played *Tipperary* and *All Through the Night*, and the man's little boy, who had been stuffing chocolate while the man was lost in a dream of melody, was sick over the rail of the steamer.

When the boat docked again, the sun was going down and it was now or never for the *Daily Amazer*.

'Are you afraid?' Carrie asked her father, as they went up in the lift.

'Jerome Fielding fears nothing and nobody.' He threw out his chest. He was wearing his jersey with *The Lady Alice* across it to show he was a genuine sailor. Two model girls in the lift with make-up cases and three-inch false eyelashes stared at the gold ring in his ear.

'To be perfectly honest with you . . .' The editor of the *Daily Amazer* was a bald pink man like an overgrown baby. 'To be perfectly honest with you . . .'

He paused and looked at Carrie's father over his rosy finger-tips. Carrie and Lester sat on the edge of their chairs. Carrie was biting what was left of her finger-nails. Her father had none to bite, because he had pruned them down with a jack knife, but he was nervous enough to blurt out, 'Will you buy me a boat?'

16

'To be perfectly honest ...' The editor paused again, watching like a cat with a mouse. 'No.'

'But look here, sir!' That was a bad sign. When Carrie's father started to call people Sir, he was either hurt or angry. 'I've come all the way from the Falkland Isles—'

'And I'd like to see you go back there.' The editor smiled and made his eyes twinkle, as if he had practised on his grandchild. 'But not alone.'

'But look here, sir, I don't want a crew. I'm a lone sailor.'

'Lone sailors don't make very pretty pictures, Mr Fielding. And there's too many of 'em. Penny a dozen, if you ask me, luffing round the world in a beard and a pair of torn shorts, most boring thing you ever saw. But girls . . . girls are what our readers want to see over the breakfast kippers. Now if you were to take a pretty girl with you through the Seven Seas—'

'I'm a married man!' Carrie's father stood up. His black beard wagged in outrage. He put his finger through his gold earring and tugged it. Sign of outrage.

'What does your wife look like?' The editor looked up at him, with his eyes twinkled almost out of sight.

'Now you're talking.' Carrie's father let go of his earring, and his white teeth came through the beard in a slow, broadening grin. He took out his wallet. He had an old picture of Carrie's mother that had been a quarter of the way round the world with him. It had been taken years ago when she was on the stage, a glowing girl with a cloud of bright golden hair.

'Whee-ew!' The editor whistled. 'Would she go?'

Oh poor Mum – no! Carrie thought, but her father said proudly, 'She'll go anywhere with me.'

'Take *her* with you and a good camera,' the editor said, 'and we'll buy you a boat at least.'

'And buy my story?' The fortune of Jerome Fielding spilled through his imagination like gold doubloons of pirate treasure.

'To be perfectly honest . . . perhaps. Can you write?'

'My dear good chap.' There was no more calling him Sir. 'I can do anything.'

With *The Lady Alice* swelling on his chest, he ran with Carrie and Lester down six flights of stairs, because he was too excited to wait for the lift. Out on to the Thames Embankment where he ran among the pigeons, startling old ladies with toy dogs on leads. Secretaries sitting on the benches looked up from magazines and smiled. A Pomeranian dog broke away from its lady and ran with him, yapping its applause.

Just before they went into the station to catch their train home, they saw a big blue plumbing van belonging to his rich brother Uncle Rudolf. On the side was Uncle Rudolf's crest, a crown and crossed water pipes, and his Latin motto, 'Princeps Plumbarium', the Prince of Plumbers.

Carrie's father ran ahead of the van to a crossing, and stepped out into the street with his hand raised. He swaggered across, to show the van driver, or himself, or someone, that he didn't need any money from the Prince of Plumbers.

Oh poor Mum! Carrie kept thinking. 'Oh, poor Mum, she won't want to go.' At World's End, she and Lester told the others what had happened in London, with Lester acting out the parts of the editor of the *Daily Amazer* and Carrie's father and even the old ladies with toy dogs. 'Oh poor Mother, she's not strong enough yet. Oh poor Dad.'

'Stop being sorry for everyone,' Tom said. 'It's insulting. Let them work it out somehow by themselves.'

'That's what I heard Dad say to Mother when I took Dog Tom into school and he ate the exam questions and Mrs Bloomers rang the police,' Michael said wonderingly. 'What's the point of being a grown-up if people are still going to talk about you as if you were a child?'

'None,' Em said.

Mother was shopping in the village when they got back from London. When Carrie was in the stable yard, she saw her coming down the lane. She was not the golden girl in the photograph any more. She was almost twenty years older

18

than that, and paler and thinner and more tired. The readers of the *Daily Amazer* would not see a glowing girl over their tea and kippers. They would see Carrie's mother.

As she came past the barn, her father ran down the front path, which was made of flat millstones set into the grass, jumping from stone to stone, the way the children did. He leaped the grassy ditch at the edge of the road instead of stepping on the stone bridge.

'I'm going to make my fortune!' he shouted. 'You're going to sail round the world with me!'

Mother had opened her mouth to say, 'Oh no!' Then she looked at his eager, grinning face, and spread her startled mouth into a smile. 'All right,' she said. 'I'll go with you.'

Four

So they were on their own again. Their father and mother went to live on the coast where the new boat was being fitted for the voyage. Tom, Carrie, Em and Michael were alone again with the animals.

'Are you sure you'll be all right?' Mother had asked, but only because she was looking for an excuse not to sail round the world. She knew they loved to live like this. No grown-ups. Just animals. Everyone equal, with an equal right to live their own kind of way. Tom as head of the house, because every herd must have a leader.

'Are you sure I should go? Michael's so young...'

'It is your duty,' Michael said, as if he were years older than her. 'By your hustbin's side.'

'I sometimes wish my husband's side would stay on dry land,' she sighed. 'But you can't change men.'

She wrote from the coast that to get her fit for the Seven Seas, their father was going to make her walk two miles a day uphill.

'How will she get down?' Michael asked Em, but she picked up her black cat like a tray, kicked open the door and stamped in boots, kicking the backs of the stairs, up to her room. She had started to flatten down her curly hair again with socks and woollen hats. She missed her father more than anyone.

Carrie missed them both, when she thought about it, but she had things on her mind. The night they got back from London, a storm of rain had washed away any hoof print the chestnut horse might have made in the lane or in the fields. She and Lester had searched in vain. They rubbed a cloth in one of the hoof marks in the vegetable garden and held it to Perpetua's nose.

'Seek!' they told her. She was supposed to be half pointer, but she didn't point at anything. She was going to have puppies again. It was her life's work.

Carrie could not get the beautiful horse out of her mind. The delicate head with the half moon white star, the small nervous ears laid back – from fear, not vice. The strong short back and fine legs. He had some Arab in him, perhaps some New Forest. He looked well fed and well groomed. Kept right, but treated wrong. *What were they doing to him now?*

One day before school started again, she went for a long ride with Mr Mismo. His name was Mr Mossman but Michael had called him Mismo, and it stuck.

He was the dairy farmer down the lane at the edge of the village. He grazed his cows in the field on the other side of their hill, and he was their best friend. He had 'lent' them the goat and the ram, and never asked for them back. He had given Michael two chickens called Diane and Currier, and later, some fertile eggs to hatch. He gave Em a pair of yellow ducklings. He gave all of them a lot of advice about horses and dogs and cats and birds and everything you could think of. Some of it worked. Some of it didn't.

He told Carrie how to ride, although she actually rode better than he did. He sat on the back of his saddle with his legs stuck out and his elbows pumping, at the same time

He sat on the back of his saddle with his legs stuck out and his elbows pumping

telling Carrie, 'Ride into your knee ... drop the hands ...
push him into the bit ... legs, girl, legs!'

He was shaped like one of his own milk churns, with a
broad red face and a bush of grey hair on which a tweed hat
rode unsteadily, turned up all round, with a blue jay's
feather in the band. When he rode, the hat was always falling
off, or getting snatched off by twigs, and Carrie had to get off
John and pick it up, because if Mr Mismo got off, he
couldn't get on again without a mounting block.

His horse was about the same shape as he was, a porridge-
coloured mare with a short fat tail and a stiff, hogged mane
that Mr Mismo would neither grow out nor clip short. It
stood straight up like a chariot horse, making her neck look
thicker than it was already.

At the end of the neck, she had a broad heavy head with a
Roman nose like a moose. On the end of her solid legs she
had huge flat feet that splayed mud out sideways. Mr Mismo
said that she had been the greatest hunter across country of
her day. He was very fond of her. Her name was Princess
Margaret Rose, because he was very fond of the royal
family too.

Carrie rode behind him down a long track through a wood.
He and his horse were both the same shape from the back.
He cantered, splashing up mud and wet leaves. Squirrels
scuttled up trees, rooks shouted the alarm from the treetops,
and blue jays went into a frenzy of scolding.

Carrie rode on a loose rein, with a poem running in her
head to the rhythm of John's canter.

> *Death – light of Spain – hurrah!*
> *Love – light – of – Af – rica!*
> *Don – John – of Aus – tria*
> *Is ri – ding to – the sea.*

Don John of Austria had been John's official name when
she took him to a show, 'Number fifty-two – Caroline Fielding riding Don John of Austria!' The brush, the rails, the
gate, the wall – she would never forget it.

She cantered half in a dream. The back of John's ears rose and fell, his mane flopped to the rhythm.

He shakes – the pea-cock gar – dens as he ri – ses – from – his ease.

And – he strides – a – mong the tree – tops—

Mr Mismo stopped suddenly, elbows out and up. John ran into Princess Margaret's tail, and Mr Mismo gave Carrie a short lecture on keeping her distance.

'You crowd like that at a show,' he said, 'and they'll put you out of the ring.'

Carrie handed him up his hat, which had fallen off when he stopped, and got back on John. 'I'm not going to any more shows.'

At the show they had been to, where John was Don John of Austria, people had laughed, because he didn't look like the other grand expensive horses. They stopped laughing when he jumped – the brush, the rails, the gate, the wall – all the huge jumps. He would have had a clear round if Carrie had not lost her head and her balance at the last jump and fallen off and wrecked everything, including the triple bar.

'Broke three bars in one go,' Mr Mismo chuckled. 'They'll be glad not to see *you* again, old dear.'

'It's not that. John's had a hard life. He was almost dead when I found him.' She looked sideways at Mr Mismo as they came out of the wood and trotted down a cart track. She still did not know how much he knew, or guessed, about the kidnapping of John. 'It's not fair to ask him to jump those awful jumps just because I want to win.'

'You credit a horse with too much feeling,' Mr Mismo said, slapping Princess on her broad oatmeal rump. 'Always have.'

'If a horse is turned out in a field where there are jumps,' Carrie said, 'have you ever seen him jump them on his own?'

'Too stupid.'

'Too clever.'

'Well, I hope they're cleverer than we are,' Mr Mismo said. They had jogged twice round the edge of a large ploughed field without finding a way out. The only gate was padlocked. They could not even find the place where they came in, plunging through a thicket, Princess breaking through like a tank.

Because Mr Mismo did not want to say he had come the wrong way, he had to find a way out. They jogged round the field again until they found the easiest place, a gap in the hedge, with a hurdle across.

'Think you and that five-legged nag can lep that?' he asked.

Mr Mismo had given Carrie plenty of jumping advice, but she had never seen him jump. If they met a fallen log in the woods, Princess trotted over it, lifting her large feet high, as if she were trotting in the sea. If there was a proper jump across the track, Mr Mismo would say, 'Ladies first', and pull behind, so that Carrie wouldn't see him ride round the jump.

If Princess Margaret had really been the finest cross-country horse of her day, the gap in the hedge would be nothing to her, but she and John, having put their noses to the hurdle, had now put their noses together to discuss whether it was all right for Mr Mismo.

'They're talking about us,' Carrie said. 'They're talking about the way we ride.'

'Oh stow it, chump.' Mr Mismo was nervous about the jump. 'Horses don't talk about us.' He never liked it when Carrie said they did, although it was often obvious, after a ride, that John and Princess Margaret Rose were swapping notes.

'Who's going first?'

'I'll show you the way,' said Mr Mismo gallantly. Red in the face, his hat tipped forward and his arms working like pistons, he wheeled Princess round, gave her a whack with his whip, and charged through the plough at the low hurdle, growling as if it were a dangerous enemy.

'Hup!' he grunted, a moment after Margaret Rose had already taken off. She went hup and over. Mr Mismo leaned far back in the saddle. One hand flew up off the reins as if he were calling a cab. His hat fell off. Princess landed on the edge of a blind ditch, stumbled, recovered with a heave like an elephant coming out of a mud bath, and trotted quietly off across the next field.

With her stirrups swinging and her reins in loops. Mr Mismo was sitting in the ditch with his grey hair on end and his crimson cheeks blown out.

'Always hang on to your reins, old chump,' he had told Carrie every time she fell off. 'Break a leg, break your neck, whatever you want, but always hang on to your reins.'

'Are you all right?' she called across the hedge.

'Go after my horse!' he shouted in answer.

He scrambled out of the way. Carrie gave John three strides and he jumped the hurdle, stretched himself cleverly to land clear of the ditch, and cantered after Princess without breaking stride. Carrie looked back and saw Mr Mismo sitting on the ground with his enormous boots stuck out in front of him and his whip in his hand, beating the ground in rage.

Five

When Margaret Rose heard John behind her, she broke into a canter. She put on speed as he increased his, dodging among bushes so that Carrie could not get alongside to grab the flying reins. With any luck, the mare would put her foot through them and have to stop, or fall down. She did put her great flat foot through them, clear through, and galloped on with the rein round her elbow.

If the field had been bigger, John would have caught her, but just as he was coming up on her left, she switched to the right, plunged into a wood and was gone among the trees, cracking dead branches, crashing through the under-growth, tearing off her stirrups. With any luck, she'd get caught up, but the luck was all with Margaret Rose. Somehow she got through the wood, twisting and turning and boring her way through.

Torn at by brambles, ducking under low branches, swerving round trees, John and Carrie followed her. When they came out on the other side, with half the wood in their mane and hair, the mare had clattered across a road and into a field of turnips. A man in the turnip field shook his fist and yelled at her, and shook his fist and yelled at Carrie, pounding after.

Princess went through someone's back garden, dragging down a laundry line, jumped a garden seat, and clattered out on to a main road with a line of baby clothes trailing from her saddle. The mother of the baby ran out of her house, flapping her apron and screaming. A car came to a screeching halt. When Carrie and John came through a gate on to the road, cars were stopped in both directions. Princess was standing in the middle of the road. A man had got out of his car, waving his arms and shouting. She shied away from him. A car hooted at her. She kicked a dent in its front wing.

Carrie jumped off and hooked John's reins over the gatepost. 'Never tie your horse up by the reins if you don't want to walk home,' chanted the remembered voice of Mr Mismo, far behind now and probably walking home himself.

'Come on, Princess. Come here, old girl.' Carrie held out her hand and whistled Mr Mismo's whistle, the notes of a blackbird's call. The mare stood still, pricked her ears as far forward as lop-ears can prick, and started towards Carrie. Just before she was close enough to reach the reins, a helpful man got out of a car, banging the door like a shot gun. Princess jumped, spun round, squeezed between two cars and galloped away down the road with a drum-rattle of hoofs.

John and Carrie went after her on the grass verge, with everyone shouting advice at them, and the mother of the baby weeping with her apron over her face, because half a week's laundry had gone with Princess Margaret Rose.

26

When Carrie at last caught up with her, it was strange country. She had never been on this road, never seen this square stucco house with the gravelled drive and the neat painted stable and pasture fence.

Princess had stopped on the brow of a hill with her head up, watching a horse in the pasture. Carrie came beside her and caught her reins easily, then got off, while the two horses put their noses down to the grass as casually as if the whole chase had been an everyday game.

There was a girl with the horse. A good-looking girl with smooth hair, clean yellow riding breeches and glossy boots. She was holding the horse on a halter and chain. He looked nervous, backing away from her, but she stroked his neck and petted him until he stood still and dropped his head, then she suddenly pulled back her arm and hit him hard behind the ears with the end of the chain.

He reared and pulled away, but she hung on, wearing gloves, while he wheeled round her, his small ears laid back. It was the chestnut horse that Michael had found in the vegetable garden.

Carrie led John and Princess up to the white paddock fence. The girl had taken sugar out of her pocket, and was holding it out towards the chestnut horse, talking to him, coaxing him. Was she going to do the same thing again – pet him and make much of him, and then suddenly hit him?

'Hi!' Carrie was younger than the girl, but she couldn't stand there and say nothing. 'Don't treat that horse like that, you'll ruin him!' she called across the field.

'That's the whole idea,' said the girl. She let go of the chain, throwing it across the horse's neck hard, so that he shied away in terror. She came towards Carrie. She had a swaggering way of walking, strutting in her shiny boots as if she owned the world, her face a mixture of pride and bad temper.

'You *want* to ruin him?' Carrie stared. Perhaps the girl was mad. She had put one hand into the pocket of her riding breeches. Perhaps she would whip out a gun and drill Carrie

27

and John and Princess Margaret Rose right between the eyes.

The girl came up to the fence and looked at Carrie and the two horses with great contempt. 'What's it got to do with you?' Her way of talking was just as conceited as her way of walking. 'What do you want?'

'Nothing. My friend's horse got loose, and I had to catch her.'

'Fell off and let go of the reins?' the girl jeered. 'Some *people*!'

'I'm glad he did,' Carrie said angrily, 'because I followed her and saw what you were doing to your horse. I could report you to the Cruelty Man, you know.' The Cruelty Man was another friend. When he didn't know what to do with animals he rescued, he brought them to World's End.

'De Cwooelty Man!' mocked the girl in baby talk. 'If you're thinking of the RSPCA, think again, you stupid little twerp. Where's the evidence?'

'I'd tell them.'

'You think they'd take *your* word?'

Carrie had met some pretty insulting girls in her life. This one took the prize. She must be the 'very rude girl' in Tom's note.

'Did you come and find your horse in our yard last week?' she asked.

'Is that your place? I might have guessed you'd come from a dump like that. Someone in your village rang the police to say they'd seen Pretty Prancer go by. So my father and I were driving round there and saw him in your yard. Not very good taste on his part.'

'Pretty Prancer? Is that his name?'

'Any objection?'

'It sounds too – too sort of fancy.'

'Well, he's not fancy any longer,' the girl said. 'My father is sending me away to some hell-hole of a school. He won't keep Prancer for me while I'm gone, so I'm going to make sure that he's so mean that nobody will buy him.'

'You can't!' The girl *was* mad. She stood there calmly saying these terrible things, as if she didn't care what Carrie thought.

'Can't what?'

'Can't ruin a horse by – by— It's – it's—' Carrie was too upset to get the words out. If only Lester were here. He would know what to say to this brute of a girl. But Lester did not go riding with Carrie, because she knew more about it. It was the only thing she could do better than him.

'Calm down, brat,' the girl said. She flicked her fingers at John's brown nose (*Bite her, John!*) and stepped back. 'It's my father's problem, not yours. I'm off to school tomorrow. He's got to spend the next three months trying to sell an unsellable horse.'

'He could sell him to me!' Carrie hadn't got any money.

'The price,' said the girl, turning away, 'will be very high. He's too tricky to be worth that now, but my father's too mean to take less than he paid for him.' As she walked off, she picked up a stone and threw it at the chestnut horse. She was not only mad, she was a devil.

By asking directions, Carrie got back on to a road she knew, and started for home. She rode John and led Princess, who pulled back sulkily, making John do all the work and almost dragging Carrie's arm out of its socket.

Twilight was closing in when they saw ahead of them a broad, dejected figure, slogging along at the side of the road. When he heard the sound of hoofs behind him, he straightened his shoulders, cocked his hat and took his whip out of his boot, holding it smartly under his arm like an army officer's cane.

Mr Mismo must have been glad and relieved to see Carrie, but all he said was, 'If you're leading on the off side, you should be on the other side of the road.'

He couldn't get on. Princess had pulled off stirrups and leathers when she plunged through the wood. He climbed on a low wall, but she kept moving away. He led her under a bank, but the soft bank crumbled under him and he could not get enough footing to push himself into the saddle.

Carrie got off to give him a leg up. Puffing and panting as much as Mr Mismo, she finally got him on to the mare's broad back.

When he was on board, he said rather stiffly, 'I owe you many thanks.'

He was embarrassed to say it, so Carrie changed the subject. 'You see,' she said, because John and Princess had their heads together as they moved off, 'they *are* talking about us.'

'Yes.' This time Mr Mismo did not deny it. 'They're saying, "Silly fat old fool",' he said glumly.

Six

Lester's mother, whose name was Mrs Figg, worked at a place where they sent lawless girls who were neither quite old enough nor quite bad enough to go to prison. The place was called Mount Pleasant. The girls called it Mount Putrid.

In the Easter holidays, Lester worked there in the garden every day. Carrie could not wait until the evening to tell him about the chestnut horse and the girl who was a mad devil, so the next morning, she rode over to Mount Pleasant on John.

Charlie came too, his thick curly mat of pale hair bouncing, his trousers fluffed out under the plume of his tail as he trotted ahead.

If you think very hard about a dog, he will eventually turn round and look at you. Carrie thought hard about Charlie. He stopped and looked round. She did it twice more, and it worked. That proved it. But when she stopped thinking about Charlie, he still turned and looked back about every hundred yards, which proved something else. Either that you couldn't make a dog do something by thinking about it. Or that you could only make him do it if he wanted to anyway.

Some of the Mount Pleasant girls were in the garden, planting cabbages. Carrie looked over the wall from John's back, and the nearest girl looked up and grinned and waved. People in the village made up terrible things about these girls, and locked their doors at night, but all the ones that Carrie had met had been friendlier than most of the girls in the village.

'Hullo, kid!' the girl said. 'Come to join the club? What did you do – steal the horse?' It was a girl called Liza, whom Carrie had met once before, going to town in Mrs Figg's car. She had a bold face and reckless eyes, with a mane of wild red hair tied with a green scarf.

'I'm looking for Lester Figg,' Carrie said.

'I think he's on the other side of the house. I'll yell.'

'No,' Carrie said. 'It's secret.'

'I got you.' Liza understood, but without begging to know the secret. 'Here, I'll hold that Derby winner and you can scout round and find him.'

She wiped her earthy hands on the seat of her jeans, jumped, caught the top of the wall, pulled herself up and swung easily over.

'They ought to have broken glass on top of that wall,' people in the village said, tut-tutting. 'Or barbed wire.' But the gates were not even locked. Any of the Mount Pleasant girls could run away, but the ones who did were always brought back.

Liza put John's reins over her arm. 'Don't hurry back.' She lit a cigarette and sat down by the wall. Charlie sat down beside her and she threw her arm over his woolly back.

Carrie clambered from the saddle to the top of the wall, jumped down on the other side and scouted round, keeping in the cover of trees and bushes, until she saw Lester washing flowerpots under the greenhouse tap. She put a broad blade of grass between her thumbs and blew gently, like a cautious owl. He looked round at once and saw her, although she was hidden behind a bush. Without making a sign, he went to the

31

back of the greenhouse, knowing she would follow.

Carrie took a deep breath, then ran as if there were snipers in the trees, and nipped into the tiny boiler room of the greenhouse, where Lester was sitting on a pile of seed-boxes.

Carrie told him about the mad devil girl and the chestnut horse. 'She's trying to ruin him for anyone else. I think she hates her father, so she's taking it out on the horse. We've *got* to save him.'

Lester listened closely, his bright eyes moving from side to side, as if her face were the page of a book. When she was finished, he didn't say, 'How dreadful!' He said, 'How marvellous!' Something like this was a challenging adventure to him, the very stuff of life.

There were two things that might happen:

1. The nervous horse might get bought by someone who would ill-treat him because they were as afraid of him as he was of them.

2. No one would buy him, and he would still be there for the mad devil to ill-treat when she came home from the hell-hole school.

'*Pretty Prancer*,' Lester said with disgust. 'I bet *she* named him.'

There were four things that Lester and Carrie might do:

1. They could buy the horse.

'With what?'

2. They could tell the Cruelty Man.

'But if there's no mark on the horse, there's nothing he can do.'

3. They could threaten the devil girl that they would tell her father what she was up to.

'She wouldn't care. And if her father's anything like her, he wouldn't either.'

4. They could steal the horse.

'Ah,' said Lester. 'Now you're talking.'

It was a week before the girl went away to school. Carrie thought about the chestnut horse all that week. *Pretty*

Prancer. What a degrading name for a horse! She could not think of him as that. Pretty Prancer. Peter Piper. Pickled Pepper. Peter Pan? Peter. He should be called Peter.

She wrote a poem on the inside of a cornflakes packet:

> *Peter, I called him, and he took the name*
> *And made it his. And though he looked the same,*
> *Nervous and proud, ears quick, legs clean and fine,*
> *His heart and life were new – for he was mine.*

She would be very quiet and patient with him, win his confidence, remember that he had been taught to fear people. He must be taught again to like them. To like Carrie. A one-man horse. A one-girl horse, who nobody else could ride, like Bucephalus, the battle charger of Alexander the Great, who never let anyone else ride him. Only the conqueror of the world.

Carrie's brother Tom found her cleaning out the end loose box. 'Got another horse coming?' he asked casually.

Carrie banged at the rafters with a broom. Lester, who believed that people and animals were the same, because they were born again after death as each other, would never sweep away a beetle or a spider which was only doing its job. 'He might be your great-uncle Ebenezer,' he said, when his mother dratted and swatted at a spider who had thought of wintering in a ceiling corner. But dusty stable cobwebs made horses cough. So Carrie swept.

'Perhaps,' she said, not looking at Tom.

He did not look at her either. 'A rescue?' He chewed a stalk of hay.

'Perhaps. Oh listen, Tom, there's a—'

She wanted so much to tell him about the devil girl and the horse, but he said, 'Don't tell me. Then I won't know.' With their father gone, Tom was man of the house, although he was still a boy. It was better if he didn't know some things until after they were done.

Seven

Lester and Carrie went to spy round the stucco house with the neat painted stable. They went across country, as the crow flies, over railway lines, through gorse commons and gaps in hedges, down narrow lanes and overgrown paths that Carrie never knew existed. When you travelled with Lester, he seemed to make up the countryside as he went along.

They saw the devil girl sulk off to school, with as much luggage as if she were the Queen going on a state visit. A dealer came to try Peter, but was so put off by the horse's nervous looks that he got back into his car without touching him. From the top of an elm on a windy day that threatened to blow them down in a shower of broken branches, Lester and Carrie watched a leathery woman ride Peter in the field.

Paper blew up. Peter shied. The woman, who did not ride as well as she thought she did, lost her temper and whipped him hard down the shoulder. He reared up and she slid off backwards and sat on the ground, still wearing the stirrups, which had slid off with her.

The girl's father called from the gate. 'No harm in him – he's just a bit fresh!'

'Fresh, my foot.' The leathery woman got up. 'He's a pig, Mr Novak. How can you— What kind of a— I'll have the law!'– She came shouting towards him. He put his coat collar up round his lined, glum face and turned away.

'Mr Novak,' Lester said in the tree. 'Mr No Thanks.'

After the leathery woman had driven away, honking her horn all down the road to annoy the neighbours, a gardener caught the horse and took off the saddle and bridle and left him in the paddock. 'Peter's not so afraid of *him*,' Lester said. 'He's probably better with men, because of that devil girl.'

34

They came down from the tree and went to the gate at the top corner of the field, away from the house. The horse watched them, head up, alert for trouble. He was a coppery chestnut, very bright, with the dazzling white crescent star and a red-gold mane and tail.

'I'm going in to get him.'

Carrie put up her hand to the gate, but Lester pulled back her arm. 'He doesn't like girls,' he said bossily. 'I'll go.'

Fury raged through Carrie like a flame. The fiercest anger is between friends.

A thin strand of wire ran round the top rail of the fence, two ends twisted together at the gate. Lester put his hand to climb over, touched the wire, yelled, jumped in the air, spun round and fell on his back as if he had been electrocuted.

He had. 'What a shock.' He propped himself on his elbows.

Carrie had been going to say nastily, 'Serve you right,' but when he grinned up at her and asked, 'Did my eyes light up?' she laughed instead.

'I'm going to find out where they switch off the current.' Lester brushed himself down, pushed back his hair, which fell forward again, went on to the road and up the gravel drive to the door of the house.

Mr Novak opened it at once, as if he had been spying behind it to catch boys. 'What do you want?'

'I'm looking for work,' Lester said. 'Could you use a boy in the stable?'

'Don't bother me.' As Mr No Thanks began to shut the door, Lester said quickly, 'I'll just look round to see if there's any odd jobs, I—'

'Buzz off,' said Mr Novak, tall and thin and beaky, not even bothering to look down at him.

When he shut the door, Lester started down the drive, then doubled back towards the stable and garage. The door opened again. 'Buzz off, I said.' The door banged.

'You try.' Lester joined Carrie behind the dustbins.

She went to the back door. A girl in an apron opened it. 'Ullo?' she said. She sounded French.

35

'Er – excuse – ex-er - excuse me, I um—' Carrie swung her hair forward, because stammering made her blush and blushing made her stammer. 'I – um, I'm – er, well, it's like this, you see. I'm from the Pony Club, you see. We're taking a – er, a – er, a count is what it is, of all the horses round here and the stables and so can I look at yours?' She ended in a rush.

The girl in the apron spread her hands. 'No Engleesh.' She had not understood a word.

They waited until the evening. The gardener came to the side door of the garage, reached in to flick a switch, then unhooked the wire on the bottom gate of the paddock. He held out a bowl of oats towards Peter, backing cautiously away until he got him into the stable, then bolted the door and snapped on a padlock. He mopped his brow with his arm and let out a sigh of relief that carried to the farmyard across the road, where Lester and Carrie were watching through the gate of an empty sty, disguised as pigs.

When they came back next day, there was a party on the lawn. The Novaks must have waited until the devil girl had gone, so that she couldn't insult the guests. People were standing about with glasses, high heels sinking into the grass, laughing and talking as if it was the finest thing in life to be standing and chattering in coats under a grey English sky. Peter was in the paddock, head and tail up, snorting at the commotion.

'Pray for rain.' Lester and Carrie went behind the dustbins. He clenched his fists and shut his eyes and screwed up his face. A few drops began to fall. 'Lester the Rainmaker.'

He watched the guests scurrying into the house with small shrieks, clutching at paper napkins on their hair, then he ran round towards the top gate of the field, while Carrie ran across the yard to the garage door. She pressed a switch – wrong one, that was the light – pressed another, and waved to Lester, waiting by the top gate.

Suppose it was the wrong switch? He trusted her. She saw

him put up his hands to untwist the wire, and shut her eyes, not daring to look, waiting for a yell.

No yell. She looked. Lester had opened the gate and was in the paddock, walking slowly towards the horse with his hand out. Peter had a halter on, but he would not let Lester reach his head, so Lester stood still in the rain with his hand out and his hair plastered down. Carrie began to climb through the fence, but he muttered to her, 'Get back. Leave him to me.' And after a while, the horse moved cautiously towards him, dropping his head, sniffed, and took the carrot. Lester stood still while the horse licked his hand, then slowly, watching him, he brought a rope from behind his back and slid it through the halter.

Carrie had walked round the outside of the fence, biting her nails with jealousy. *It doesn't matter who catches him*, her outer self said. Her inner self whined, *I wanted it to be me.*

Lester led Peter through the gate and she went up to him. He backed away, and they would have lost him if Lester had not hung on, dragged across the grass like a fisherman who has hooked a whale.

'I told you!' he said angrily, after the horse stopped. 'He doesn't like *girls*.'

He led Peter over the hill and down into a copse where they were hidden from the house and from the road. Carrie followed.

A one-girl horse! Carrie and Peter. *Nobody else could ride him*. Now she could not even lead him.

They didn't take him straight to World's End, in case Mr Novak remembered that he had run there before. They took him to an abandoned farm in a fold of the hills and left him in a cowshed for the night. Very early next morning, without waiting for Lester, Carrie went to the farm. The horse was gone. Lester had not waited for *her*. He had taken the horse away somewhere so that she couldn't have him.

All right. Carrie set her jaw. That was it then. The end of their friendship. That was the way life was. When you thought you had found someone for good, you lost them.

She sat down on the ground and threw stones into an old rain barrel. Plonk, plonk, plonk. Each plonk sent up a jet of sour green water.

'Nine out of ten. Not bad for a girl.' Lester came up behind her. Carrie scrambled up and faced him. 'What have you done with Peter?'

'What have *you* done with him?' Carrie was red with fury. Lester was white. They were both trembling.

'You wanted him for yourself!'

'*You* wanted him! Where is he?'

'Wherever you've taken him.'

'Where *you* took him!'

They hardly knew what they were saying. They stared in hate. Charlie was barking like a maniac. 'Shut up,' Carrie snapped at him. 'It's not your business.'

But he wasn't barking at them. He was round the side of the shed, barking at Peter, who had broken the halter rope and was now caught by the end of it in a tangle of bushes, trapped and sweating.

When he had quietened down, they took him home to World's End. He was less nervous today. Lester led him and Carrie walked on the other side of him, and after a while, she could put her hand on his neck. His skin was fine and thin, like thoroughbred skin. She ran her fingers up to the warmth beneath his silky red-gold mane.

Then she and Lester both said at exactly the same time, as if their minds were linked by the horse between them, 'Sorry.'

Eight

Tom came home from work, tired but content. He had helped Mr Harvey with a long and difficult operation on a dog's crushed leg. The owner, an old man with trembling

38

hands, sat in the waiting-room and wept, because another vet had told him the dog would die.

After two hours, Tom showed him his dog, bandaged and splinted, alive and feebly thumping her tail. The joy of the old man's face was still reflected in Tom's smile when he came home.

Michael ran to meet him with his speedy up-and-down limp. Tom picked him up and swung him. 'Guess what?' It was too exciting for Michael to keep. 'We've got another customer.'

'Nice-looking horse.' Tom hung the top of his long, loose body over the half door of the loose box. 'Where did you get that one?'

Lester was sitting in the manger, holding Peter and soothing him while he stamped nervously. He said nothing. Tom was Carrie's brother, not his.

Carrie was kneeling in the straw. She stood up quickly and turned round, hiding something. 'We're boarding him for someone.' She put back her hair and made an honest face.

'Anyone I know?'

'I don't think so. They live – oh, somewhere the other side of the brook.' She waved a hand vaguely.

'Good idea,' Tom said, 'if it helps to pay the feed bill. How much?'

'Well actually, they're not – I mean, I'm sorry for them, you see. They've had a lot of bad luck.'

'Oh?' Tom was smiling.

'Their son had a – had a car crash, and their daughter ran away with the milkman, and the father lost his job. As a riveter. They filled in the river instead of building a bridge.' If you told one lie, it led you into a million of them.

'How sad,' Tom said. 'Is that why you're painting their horse's legs?'

She told him then about Peter and the mad devil girl and what she had done to him.

'Oh Lord,' Tom said, 'there's no end to it.'

'But you'd have done the same as me! You said yourself,

39

*She told him then about Peter and the mad devil girl
and what she had done to him*

World's End should be a refuge for animals that had suffered—'

'That's what I mean. No end to the suffering that people cause.'

'Mr Novak may come here,' Lester said from the manger, taking a bull's eye out of his cheek and giving it to Peter. 'He'll remember that the horse was here before. But if he does, he won't find a horse with two white socks and a half moon star. Peter will have no white socks. And look.' He turned Peter's head round to show the broad white blaze that they had painted down his nose with whitewash.

'I hope I shan't be here.' Tom went off with Michael to work on their invention for brightening candle-power with angled reflectors. There was no electricity at World's End.

Bits of straw were sticking to the wet brown paint on Peter's legs. Carrie had to pick them off and put on another coat. They brought him out to inspect him in the light. The white blaze was not bad, but the legs would not have fooled an idiot, much less a glum, suspicious man like Mr No Thanks. They were the wrong colour, and the hair was matted and clinging as if Peter had been walking in a bog.

Em came across the yard with Maud, the deaf white cat, on her shoulder, and a few of Pip's children and grandchildren behind her, stalking blown straws, crouching in a hoof print, wriggling and stamping for the pounce. One of Pip's first two kittens, Julius and Caesar, had turned out to be a woman. She was now called Julia, and there were getting to be enough cats to satisfy even Em.

Last week they had given two away, but they kept coming back, and their new people were insulted and would not fetch them any more.

'What do you think of Peter?' Carrie asked Em hopefully.

'I think he looked better before.'

'But we've got to disguise him! How do you think he looks?'

'Like a horse who's had a blaze whitewashed on his face and his legs painted the wrong shade of brown.'

41

Em came closer. Peter put back his ears.

'Watch him,' Lester warned. 'He's still scared of girls.'

'Not as scared as I am of him,' Em said. But she stayed still, while Maud, who was too deaf and smug to be afraid of a horse, stood on her shoulder and stretched out her round fur head to Peter, touching noses with a little shock of cat electricity.

Peter was still jumpy and nervous, throwing up his head if you moved your hand quickly, as if he expected to be hit. But he was growing calmer all the time, more sure of them, more like he must have been before the mad devil girl got at him.

'It would be a tragedy if he had to go back there,' Carrie said. 'How else do people disguise a horse?'

'Stick on a false tail?' Em suggested.

'That long hair piece Aunt Valentina used to wear,' Carrie remembered. 'That would have done it.'

'Aunt Val . . .' Em was thinking under the wide hair-band holding down her curls. 'What was it she . . . ? Remember she was going grey, only she thought no one knew, but I found the black stuff she put on her hair, that day you were such hours in the bath and I went into her bathroom.'

'It wasn't me. *I* wasn't hours. It's not me who reads in the bath with a cat sitting on the edge drinking the water.'

'It was you that day. I beat and beat on the door, but all you did was turn the taps on. I remember it as if it was yesterday.'

'I don't remember it at all.'

'Girls,' said Lester, '*please*! That's not the point. The point is your Aunt Valentina's hair dye. What was it?'

'Black something,' Em tried to remember. 'Black Diamond . . . Black Pepper . . . Black Beauty . . . something like that.'

'*Black?*' said Carrie. 'That's it. We'll dye his legs black and his mane and tail too, and then he won't be a chestnut any more. He'll be a bay.'

'It's genius,' said Lester. 'Go down to the village and get

the stuff, and I'll start washing off this paint. Thanks, Emmie.'

'Think nothing of it.' Em went on her way with the convoy of cats. 'Any time.'

Carrie hesitated. 'I haven't got any money.'

'Tell the chemist I'll pay on Friday,' Lester said. 'Mr Evans is a friend of mine. I count pills for him.' Lester had friends everywhere, always just the kind you needed.

'For young Lester, is it?' Mr Evans rubbed his blue chin, which looked as if he ought to sell himself some of his 'Bristle-Begone' shaving cream. 'Poor lad. Is he going grey already?'

'It's for a play he's getting up,' Carrie said. 'For the old people.' When she was nervous, she always had to invent more than necessary. 'At the Golden Age Home.'

'Well . . . black, you say? There's tints and rinses. Let's see . . .' He looked along a shelf. 'Blackberry . . . Slate Mate . . . Jet Set . . . Chocolate Sundae . . . Dark Secret . . . Black Rage . . .'

He was maddeningly slow. He mumbled among the bottles. Carrie fumed, imagining Mr No Thanks already driving up the lane with his eyes peeled.

'Black Rage – please. May I have that?' She grabbed the bottle before he could start fiddling with wrapping-paper and sealing-wax, ran out of the shop, and rode furiously home on Old Red, the bicycle that went 'squee-clunk' when the pedal hit the chain guard.

The brown paint would not wash off. They tried turpentine. Peter nearly went mad. They jumped out of the stable as the turpentine reached the skin, and he thrashed round the loose box, kicking, banging, lying down and rolling to try and get rid of the burning. Lester ran to get the hose, and they sluiced his legs with cold water until the pain stopped.

'What are you doing?' Michael asked, as they were forking out the soaked straw.

'Playing the piano,' Carrie said. The adventure was getting rather grim.

The Black Rage hair dye went on quite easily, although it was hard to get near Peter's legs after the turpentine. He did look quite different. He was a bright enough chestnut to look like a bay when his legs and mane were black.

'Put a bit more on his tail.' Lester was standing back with his head on one side, like an artist considering a picture.

'Me?' Carrie thought Peter was sick of being messed about. His back was humped and his tail was clamped down.

'Sorry, I forgot.' Lester grinned happily. 'He doesn't like girls.'

Peter still was better with Lester than anyone else. Carrie was still jealous. But disguising him was all that mattered, not only for his sake, but for theirs. They had stolen a horse. If they were found out . . .

'If it's prison, I hope they send me to Mount Pleasant,' Carrie said gloomily. 'Your mother would be kind to me, at least.'

It was two days before Mr Novak arrived. He came in a very expensive car and walked up to the front door with a hat and a rolled umbrella, as if he were paying a formal call.

Nobody was at home but Carrie and Lester. When they saw the car stop, they ran upstairs into the attic and watched from the little window over the World's End inn sign, which Michael had painted with a picture of a little house sitting on the edge of the globe.

Nr Novak kept knocking on the door with the handle of his umbrella. 'Go down,' Lester said.

Carrie knew that she would blush and stammer, and Mr Novak would take her off to the police station without even having to look at Peter. 'I'm afraid.'

'So am I.'

She had never heard Lester say that. She squeezed his hand. 'Goodbye, Carrie,' he said. 'Tell them I died bravely.'

Bang, bang, on the front door. They saw the top of Mr

Novak's grey hat, with darkening spots on it. It was beginning to rain. He put up his umbrella and began to walk round the side of the house.

Lester and Carrie ran down the stairs and out through the back door, slowing to a casual walk as they saw Mr Novak under his umbrella, looking over the loose box doors. The horses were out in the meadow.

When they came up to him, he took off his hat and apologized for trespassing. They had expected an ogre, a monster, the hateful father of a hateful girl. He was rather nice. As he told them about losing the horse, they saw that the lines in his face were from worry, not bad temper.

They were able to tell him quite honestly that his horse had not run here a second time. Because he hadn't run. He had been led.

Mr No Thanks nodded, and they thought he would go. But then he looked again at Carrie and said, 'You're the girl who jumped so well at the show. Have you still got that fantastic brown horse?'

'Yes. John. Don John of Austria. He's in the meadow.'

'I'd love to see him.'

'It's raining awfully hard.'

It was coming down in sheets, but Mr Novak said, 'I don't mind if *you* don't,' and held his large umbrella up so that they could all three walk underneath it.

Carrie and Lester walked with their fingers crossed. But why be afraid? Mr Novak was looking for a chestnut with a half moon star. Peter was a bay with a long blaze.

Lester saw him first. 'Tell them,' he muttered, 'that I died bravely.'

Mr Novak bent down his head. 'What did you say?'

Lester said nothing. Carrie said nothing. Then Mr Novak looked ahead, and he said nothing.

John and Oliver and Leonora and Peter had come splashing down the hill when they heard them. They were all streaming wet, manes clinging, tails tucked in. Peter was not a bay any more. The rain had washed the Black Rage out of

45

his legs and mane and tail, and most of the whitewash off his face.

They stood in silence under the umbrella while the two horses and the pony and the donkey pushed each other jealously away from the gate.

'Is that my chestnut horse?' Mr Novak said at last, in a conversational way, as if he were asking the time.

'Some dye,' Carrie said, not caring now if he heard.

'You dyed him?' He looked down at her curiously.

'His legs and mane and tail. But it must have been a rinse, not a dye.'

'You, er—' Mr No Thanks cleared his throat. 'You stole him then?'

They nodded. Lester put out his wrists for handcuffs.

'You mean you – you *want* him?'

They stared. Something peculiar was happening to Mr Novak's face. The long lines and folds that dropped heavily downward were struggling to lift themselves into a smile. His mouth worked. His jaw clenched. Cords stood out in his neck. He suddenly let out a bellow of laughter that scattered the horses and the donkey, kicking up their heels in the puddled mud by the gate.

He was as mad as his daughter. 'It's the funniest thing that ever happened to me! Don't you see? I couldn't *give* that tricky beast away. My daughter didn't want him. Gone boy-mad. That's why I sent her away to school. But no one would buy him at any price. I thought I was stuck with him.'

'You mean—?'

'I mean,' he said, 'I'm glad to be rid of him. You can keep him if you're really sure you can handle him.'

Carrie and Lester were looking at each other without expression, seeing back to all that had happened. The spying, the planning, the electric shock, the painting, the turpentine, the Black Rage, the fear with which they had watched the top of Mr Novak's hat from the attic window. Worst of all, the moment of violent anger when they had faced each other by the abandoned cowshed. They had almost lost their friendship.

46

The rain had stopped as suddenly as it began. The sun came out and the horses began to steam.

'Take care of him,' Mr No Thanks said, as he closed his umbrella and turned away. '*She* never did.'

Nine

School started. There was no escape. Like the rising and setting of the sun, the ebb and flow of the tide, no human power could prevent the summer term.

Every morning, Carrie drove Em and Michael behind John in the brown and yellow trap, with Charlie and Moses running underneath (Perpetua was too near to having her puppies).

The dogs stayed outside the school all day, investigating the neighbourhood smells, calling in for snacks at back doors where they were known. If school was late coming out, they looked in at Michael's ground floor classroom, paws on the windowsill, tongues lolling, heads on one side, the tufts on Charlie's ears sticking out, until the class giggled itself into an uproar, and Miss McDrane lashed out right and left with a rolled-up map of Australia.

Sometimes the goat and the ram followed the trap. Lucy usually turned off at the rubbish tip, but Henry sometimes came all the way. His mild, chewing face would appear at the window. 'Mary!' the class would shout at Michael. 'Mary had a little lamb . . .'

'Shut up! Shut up!' He jammed his thumbs into his ears and screamed.

'Quiet, everybody! Qui-utt!' Miss McDrane shrieked louder than anyone.

John spent the day in the bakery stable, next to the school. The baker was a cousin of Mrs Croker, the English teacher. He let Carrie use his stable while his horse and van were out on the bread rounds. It was very convenient. Carrie fought a girl called Hazel Oddie for a desk by the window. Beyond the mustard and cress that grew in saucers of wet flannel on the sill, she could hear John blowing at hay and stamping at flies, while Mrs Croker recited poetry.

They were doing Tennyson. Mrs Croker was a mad, enthusiastic woman with wild china-blue eyes and iron-grey hair which she cut herself round a pudding basin upside down on her head. The blunt chopped ends flew out as she declaimed:

> *'Blow, bugle, blow, set the wild echoes flying,*
> *Blow, bugle, answer, echoes, dying, dying, dying.'*

She waved her short arms and whirled about the room, striding between the desks, touching people on top of the head with electric fingers.

> *'I hate the dreadful hollow behind the little wood,*
> *Its lips in the field above are dabbled with blood-red*
> *heath . . .'*

When Mrs Croker recited that poem, 'Maud', she got so worked up that Beryl Fitch, who sat at the back, kept one hand on the fire extinguisher.

> *'Birds in the high Hall garden*
> *When twilight was falling,*
> *Maud, Maud, Maud,*
> *They were crying and calling.'*

With each wail of 'Maud', she closed her eyes and put her hands to her mouth like a trumpet. The two back rows were in fits. Gloria Sweet stuffed the end of her pigtail into her mouth, went blue in the face and had to be thumped on the back by Mrs Croker.

> *'Birds in the high Hall garden* (thump)
> *Were crying and calling to her* (thump)

Where is Maud (thump), *Maud* (thump), *Maud* (thump)?
One is come to woo her (THUMP!)'

English class was the best part of school.

But school was only a half life. The real thing began when they drove home.

Up the white hill road. Through the cool fir wood at the top. Down into their own village and through the main street, with friends looking out of windows and shop doors at the sound of John's hoofs. Out past Mr Mismo's dairy farm, where he usually 'happened' to be at the gate to call out, 'Why don't *you* run underneath and let the dogs drive?' or, 'That nag is lame in all five legs!' or any of his favourite, familiar, feeble jokes.

On the wall of the stable yard, a row of whiskered cats waited for Em. As they turned in at the gate – the wheel hub missing the post by half an inch, the way John and Carrie liked to judge it – puppies bounded from everywhere, and Michael jumped down into a foaming sea of tongues and yelps and waving tails.

From the hen house, Diane and Currier called boring news about eggs they had laid, or could have laid, or might yet lay if the fancy took them. The goat looked up from the rubbish heap, necklaced with shredded plastic bags. Leonora let out a terrible bray that sent the birds circling up to the tops of the trees. Peter and Oliver Twist greeted John from the meadow, and John sent back a trumpet call, usually in Carrie's ear, as she was backing him into the cart shed.

Em and the cats went off to start cooking something. Michael and the puppies went off to invent something (they were working on furniture made out of old horseshoes). Carrie fed John, and turned him out to roll in the muddiest place he could find. When it had been raining, he came up plastered solid like a plated dinosaur.

Before she turned John out, Carrie brought Peter in, or she would never have caught him. Peter was difficult to catch, among the other things that were difficult to do with him.

He was, as Mr Mismo said, 'a chancy ride'. You never knew what would happen. He was very quick and responsive, sometimes unexpectedly so. He might stand like a rock, pretending to stare at something on the horizon. Suddenly at the slightest pressure of legs, he would be over the top of the hill with you before you could shorten your reins.

He had once been well schooled, but the hard-handed treatment of Mr Novak's mad devil daughter had made him nervous and jumpy.

'He's unsure,' Mr Mismo said, after Peter had shied at nothing, right across the road, and dumped Carrie in a thorn hedge.

'Not half as unsure as I am.' She picked out the larger thorns, and remounted, Peter circling wildly, and bumping into Princess Margaret Rose, who bit him. Even Mr Mismo's steady old cob was touchy when she was out with Peter.

Carrie rode him in John's snaffle bridle. It was the only one they had, except for Oliver's small bridle which Michael had paid for by selling manure round the housing estates.

'Get him collected!' Mr Mismo shouted after her, as Peter trotted off fast. 'Bring him back to you and use your legs to get him on the bit!' She did all the correct things, that worked with John, but Peter chucked the bit up into the corners of his mouth, or yawed down with it, pulling her half out of the saddle, and finally shied at a non-existent bogey in a cabbage field and put Carrie on the ground again.

'You could pull out all his eyelashes,' Mr Mismo said helpfully. 'That's the old Indian trick with a shying—'

Getting on, Carrie had kicked Peter by mistake, and was away into the middle distance before Mr Mismo could finish his sentence, and gather up his reins to follow at Princess Margaret's rolling, beer barrel canter.

The odd thing was - not odd to Lester, but odd to Carrie - that Lester had more success with Peter than she did. He rode all wrong, sloppily, on a loose rein, uncollected, dreamy. Peter went quietly and did not shy. Lester rode him like an Indian, like a Roman, like an Arab in the desert, bareback, fingers twined in the mane, relaxed and at one with his horse, as Carrie was only able to be in the waking dream of her own invention when she galloped with John up to the Star where the horses of history grazed.

One night when she could not sleep, she rode Peter up to the Star to show him off.

Some of the horses were a bit huffy at first. They preferred to see a plain horse like John, who was no threat to their pride. Peter moved among them like a king, showing off, picking up his feet prettily, head up, neck flexed at the perfect point behind the ears.

Carrie sat him easily, like Lester, fingers in his golden mane, legs close to the warm strength of him. There were no saddles or bridles on the Star. No fences. No gates, except the one at the edge, for people who had died to lean on and chew grass while they waited for their own horse to come galloping over the Elysian Fields.

She saw an old lady there in a long, old-fashioned riding habit, top hat and veil, bunch of violets in her buttonhole, and saw her old hunter canter stiffly up and drop his nose into her small blue-veined hand. The old lady stood on the gate and mounted, side saddle without a saddle, and they moved off as they had once moved off after hounds to the first covert, going on together – where? Carrie would not find that out until she had died herself.

She saw a young man who had been killed in a war, somewhere on earth. He was waiting for the pony he had ridden when he was a boy. The pony was a blue roan with a broad speckled face. It was too small for him now, so they walked away, the young man with an arm thrown over the pony's thick mane which flopped on both sides from years of waiting, head down to the sweet grass, until his friend arrived.

'I know that chestnut.' Some horses were talking about Peter. 'Didn't I see you once at the Pony Club Combined Event?' a Thoroughbred asked. 'What's your name?'

'Peter.'

51

Peter, I called him, and he took the name
And made it his . . .

Carrie and he were not going to let on that he had ever been called Pretty Prancer.

'No, it wasn't that.' The Thoroughbred had a conceited, superior manner, flicking his tail in people's faces and laying back his slender ears if a common horse came too close. 'Something soppy. My Fairy Prince. Beauty of Basingstoke – one of those ghastly names those brats think up when Daddy buys them an expensive horse.'

'It wasn't me.'

'It was. I remember your dressage. Very fine, in spite of a ham-fisted girl with a lead seat and legs like bowling-pins. I've got it – Pretty Prancer. Ugh!' He made the kind of noise a horse would make if it could vomit.

Carrie and Peter jumped off the edge of the Star and drifted back to World's End, riding the night sky.

Ten

'It's the snaffle that's wrong,' she told Lester, after trying for half an hour to make Peter change leads in a figure of eight.

'It feels all right to me.' Lester was sitting on the fallen tree in the flat corner of the meadow. The monkey sat beside him, picking under the bark for wood lice.

'He's always on the wrong lead with you.'

'It doesn't matter.'

'It *does* matter.'

'Why does it?' Lester had made a daisy chain. He put it round Joey's neck and the monkey tore it off and ate it.

'It just does.' Lester understood all things about life, but it was impossible to explain the finer points of riding to someone who did not care. 'And anyway,' she said, 'I think he's been schooled in a curb.'

'If you're going to put a curb on him,' Lester stood up and the monkey jumped into his arms, not wanting to be left, 'you're not going to ride him.'

'Who says?'

'I do.'

'He's half my horse.'

'The back end.'

'Since when?'

'Since you said you want to put a curb in the front end.'

When Lester had gone home, Carrie went down the lane to Mr Mismo's farmhouse and knocked on the back door. He opened it with a napkin in one huge hand and his mouth full of kippers. He and Mrs Mismo were having their tea.

'Just come at the right time. Come in, old dear, and sit down.'

'Come in, Carrie, I've got some hot scones for you!' Mrs Mismo called. She was sure they were starving at World's End. She often came down with cakes and buns and home-made bread.

'No thanks. I can't stay. Em's made cottage pie.'

'Rather you than me.' Mr Mismo made a face. Em had once made cottage pie with tinned dog food, because it looked so good.

'Could I borrow that pelham?' Mr Mismo had a col-lection of old bits decorating the walls of his back hall, in-stead of calendars or mottoes.

'For Don John of Hoss-tria?' Mr Mismo took down the steel pelham bit, burnished with sand and chain-cloth in the old grooms' way before stainless steel. 'He's got a snaffle mouth, if nothing else.'

'I want to try Peter in it.'

'Go easy then. This is a mite severe.' He ran his broad red finger down the long cheek of the bit. 'He's touchy with his head. Been jabbed in the mouth too many times, if you ask me.'

'You said I had good hands.'

53

'I've seen better.' He had always seen better. 'I knew a lady once who rode a seventeen hand horse on a silk thread.'

Next day after school, Carrie hurried to put the pelham into John's bridle and fit it on Peter. Michael was in the meadow with the pony, so she got on Peter in the yard and walked round, not touching his mouth. He fussed with the bit and shook his head, clinking the curb chain. When she pulled him in gently, he resisted. She pulled a little harder. When he felt the pinch of the chain under his chin, he threw up his head and backed wildly, through the manure heap, knocking over a wheelbarrow, scattering chickens and pigeons, and missing by inches the sun-bathing tortoise.

Yesterday he would not back at all. Now he wouldn't stop. He finally backed himself into the wall, crashing a pile of flowerpots, and Carrie got quickly off. What now?

Lester turned up at World's End most afternoons, dropping casually out of a tree, or coming through a hedge from the wrong direction, or hopping down from the back of a passing lorry. He had said, 'If you're going to put a curb on him, you're not going to ride him.' So when Carrie heard the scolding of blue jays from the corner of the beech wood, which meant that Lester was coming through that way, she led Peter out of the gate and into the field across the lane, mounted, used her legs as hard as she dared, and rode off out of sight round the hill.

She rode Peter with a very light contact, hardly feeling his mouth. He flexed, stepped out, trotted beautifully, with his head steady and his fine ears forward. She was right! She rode in joy, singing.

They hopped through the gap in the hedge at the top of the hill, and on to the huge flat expanse of grass that had once been a Fighter airfield, long ago in the War. Peter took hold. She pulled him in. As soon as he felt the curb, he started to back again. He backed into the hedge and stopped, trampling, nervous and excited, between desire to gallop, and fear of the bit.

'Come on, Peter!' Carrie used her legs and slackened the

reins. With a jet-propelled thrust of his quarters, he was off with her, over the broken macadam of the old runway, past the tumbledown Air Force sheds, across another runway, galloping much too fast over the long uneven grass.

Carrie had once ridden a racehorse, and found out there was no way to stop. If you pulled, the racehorse went faster, leaning against your hands. The same thing was happening with Peter. The more she pulled, the more he pulled against the hated bit, fighting away from the pain, setting his jaw and his neck so that she couldn't even turn him in a circle.

At the top of the airfield, there was a narrow track under trees to the common. Carrie leaned forward under the clutching branches. Peter went faster. He burst out on to the common, swerving round gorse bushes, jumping them, floundering through a boggy place and out on to firm ground on the broad track that led to the road. Carrie pulled. She prayed. She begged Peter. To her shame, she realized afterwards, she had shouted and wept.

Being run away with is a black madness of despair. The horse is your fate, and your fate is out of control. Galloping crazily, Peter dashed her under a tree at the edge of the common, slid down a bank, landed on the road to the roar of a motor-cycle and stumbled and fell as the motor-cycle swerved, just missing, and roared on.

Peter scrambled up at once. A few yards away, Carrie got up slowly, shaken and battered, and shook her fist after the dwindling motor-cyclist. It wasn't his fault. But he might have stopped. But she was glad he hadn't. One side of her face was scorched and grazed. The eye was closing. Dirt was in her mouth. Her teeth felt loose, and her brain felt looser. Her legs felt as if she had been in bed for a week.

She would have to lead Peter home. She limped over to him and reached for the reins. He flung up his head and cantered off down the road, stirrups bumping and flying.

He landed, stumbled and fell as the motor cycle swerved

Eleven

She walked for a long time. When anyone came by, she turned away her face and stood still, so that they would not see her limp. She felt that she must look as dreadful as she felt. They would rush her off to the hospital. Doctors would prod her bones. They would pull down the blinds and say she had concussion. It would all be more than she could bear.

Trudging along with her head down and aching, her knee hurting so badly that she began to be sure that she would never run, or even walk again, she thought dark and bitter thoughts, while low clouds swirled up the valley and began to spread downwards in fine misty rain. She would be a cripple for life. She would be in a wheel chair, her shoulders powerful as a man from turning the wheels. She would be like that lady who went on riding after a crippling fall in a point-to-point. They would have to dig a pit for John to walk into, so that she could slide on to his back from her wheel chair. Would she get a medal? What for? She had been a fool, not a heroine.

She heard the sound of hoofs without looking up. Who cared? Other people went riding. Other people had horses. Quiet, well-mannered horses who couldn't canter a hundred yards without blowing and slowing, let alone gallop against a curb for miles and miles.

The hoof beats came nearer, came round a corner. Carrie turned and began to walk in the other direction, so that they would not see her grazed and swollen face.

'Carrie!'

She turned. It was Michael on Oliver. Lester was with him, riding Peter bareback, in a rope halter.

'You're going the wrong way,' Michael said with interest. 'Were you knocked silly?'

Carrie hung her damp hair, but Lester got off and came to her, leading Peter, and put her hair gently back behind her ears to see her face.

'You really did it this time.' His dark eyes searched the damage.

'What does it look like?'

'As bad as it feels.'

Michael was chattering away, asking a hundred questions, whistling at her mashed face, predicting that she had broken her knee, lost the sight of her eye, would catch murder from Tom, would have to wear a veil for the rest of her life, like that old lady at the Golden Age Home who had fallen into the fire . . .

Lester did not say anything. He gave Carrie a leg up on to Peter's short strong back, and hopped up in front of her. Clinging round his thin waist, she was too weak and dizzy to ask him if he thought it was safe to ride double on Peter.

Michael jogged beside them on Oliver's short spry legs, trotting when they walked fast, rising very high and quick in the saddle like an animated toy, asking questions which Carrie only half heard, drowsily, with her head lolling to the rhythm of Peter's long walk.

When they were almost home, she heard a voice which must be her own, thick out of a swollen mouth.

'If Peter goes so well for you in a halter,' she said to the back of Lester's dark alert head, 'it won't matter only having one bridle. We can ride together now.'

When Tom came home, he went to the village for the doctor. They had tried to stay clear of him. They were afraid that he might say they were undernourished or neglected, like Mrs Loomis and Miss McDrane at the school, who were always suspicious of what went on at World's End.

But the doctor was easy. Fairly young, small and thin with round spectacles and a pale tired face. If anyone was under-nourished, he was.

He didn't say anything about neglect, or too many animals and too little house-cleaning. He looked at Carrie and murmured, and felt her knee gently, and drew the curtains and told them to let him know if she threw up.

When he went away, he must have telephoned their mother, because Carrie woke from a confused sleep to find her sitting by the bed.

'How funny,' Carrie said. 'I used to sit by your bed when you were in the hospital, and watch you sleeping. Your eyes moved under the lids like marbles.'

'Did they?' Her mother laughed. She looked brown and healthy. 'How unattractive.'

'No. I was glad, because then I knew you weren't dead.'

Living on their own was very fine. But having Mother there was fine too.

Em and Michael took care of the horses, and Carrie lay under the window with the curtains blowing, and nothing to do but pick bits of gravel out of the graze on her face. When she asked her mother for a mirror, her eye was black and blue and green and her cheek was like a squashed tomato, so she didn't ask for the mirror again.

Her mother read horse books and poetry to her. She read 'Reynard the Fox', and 'Right Royal':

> . . . And a voice said, 'No,
> Not for Right Royal.'
>   And I looked, and, lo!
> There was Right Royal, speaking, at my side.
> The horse's very self, and yet his hide
> Was like, what shall I say? like pearls on fire,
> A white soft glow of burning that did twire
> Like soft white-heat with every breath he drew.
>
> . . . And I was made aware
> That, being a horse, his mind could only say
> Few things to me. He said, 'It is my day,
> My day, today; I shall not have another.'
>
> And as he spoke he seemed a younger brother
> Most near, and yet a horse, and then he grinned

59

And tossed his crest and crinier to the wind,
And looked down to the Water with an eye
All fire of soul to gallop dreadfully.

Michael read to her from an old book called *Bunny Brothers*, which he had found in the attic among musty clothes and sagging tennis racquets.

'Mrs Bunny had lad the bake fast, and now she saw very busy tiring the podridge over the fire to keep it form bunning.'

Em came up the stairs to bring her a few cats for bed company, and to read her a piece out of the local newspaper. It said that a lady called Miss Christabel Mayberry, who lived on the gorse common, had seen the ghost of the famous Headless Horseman, who was supposed to have broken his neck hundreds of years ago, riding over the edge of the quarry. Miss Mayberry thought it was a disaster warning against sending men to the moon.

At night, Carrie rode John up the Star and took the piece out of the newspaper, to show that she and Peter were famous.

An old bag of bones called Gunpowder started to tell a long-winded story of how he and his rider, Ichabod Crane, had been chased by a goblin on a black steed, carrying its head in front of it on the saddle.

'And when we came to the bridge . . .' The old horse's eyes bulged. He swung his bony head from side to side. 'It threw – it threw its head at us!'

'Oh, come on now, Gun.' Marocco, the famous trick horse from Elizabethan times, had heard Gunpowder's hair-raising story too often. 'You know the goblin was only a man with a cloak over his head, carrying a pumpkin.'

'You spoiled my story.' Gunpowder grumbled away, mumbling at the grass with his long yellow teeth.

Carrie talked to Marocco about the strangeness of Peter going so well with Lester, and without a bit.

'It's not so strange,' Marocco said. 'All this ironmongery they put in your mouth . . . Often, the less you put on a horse, the better he'll go for you. The American Indians knew that.'

'But *I* couldn't hold Peter in a halter,' Carrie said. 'I think he's really Lester's horse.' On the Star, you could say the truth, and it didn't hurt.

'Ah, yes,' said Marocco. 'For every person, there is one horse. For every horse, there is one person.'

John turned his head round and nudged his soft oatmeal nose at Carrie's bare toe. 'They just have to find each other,' he said.

While she was in bed, Carrie wrote that down. Her mother brought her a notebook, and she began to write down other things that she thought, or had found out about horses. She stuck a label on the front:

'*Carrie's Horse Book*'.

When Em found out about this, she got out a diary which she had stopped keeping after the first two weeks of January, and started her own book:

'*Esmeralda's Book of Cats*'.

When Michael heard about that, he took a marbled exercise book from the store cupboard at school and began a book of laws and truths about dogs.

It was called: '*Micheal's Dog Lores*'.

Twelve

'Why do they make the summer term the longest, when summer is the best part of the year?'

Michael filled his chest full of warm new air and sighed deeply. They were driving to school on a glorious morning, the fields golden with buttercups, white flowers foaming in the hedges, the village gardens bright as the illustrations on seed packets.

It was a day to be outdoors. A day to be under the sky.

Not under a low ceiling, freckled from hundreds of ink darts, crouched over a desk scarred with years of other people's initials and rude sayings.

'Only two more months.' Carrie slapped the reins on John's back. He turned one ear round to her, but kept his steady pace, the breeching flopping, right, left, as his quarters moved.

'I don't think I can last that long.'

'What's the matter – Miss McDrane been making trouble again?'

Michael nodded. 'But don't tell Mother,' he added quickly.

Mother got very worked up about Miss McDrane. She called her, 'That woman at the school – McGutter, McSewer, McCesspool – what's her horrid name?'

Miss McDrane wrote on the bottom of Michael's papers, 'Facts: D. Spelling: Z. Grade – N' in green, insulting ink.

In the alphabet which Mother and Michael had invented with different and more useful letters, he could get Spelling: A. 'I wish I could teach you myself,' Mother often sighed.

'They'd put you behind bars,' he said. 'It is the Law.'

As they turned into the street where the school was, and saw the corrugated tin roof of the cloakroom flashing silver in the sun Michael made a finger against the evil eye. 'Miss McDrane says I am allergic to learning. That's a terrible thing to say to anyone.'

'Do you know what it means?'

'No.'

'It means – like Lester can't have pets because his father is allergic to anything with fur on it. It makes him ill.'

'Well so does *She* make me ill,' Michael said.

When they had unharnessed John and settled him in the bakery stable, Carrie said, 'I'm going to talk to that woman.' When their parents were away, they had got used to taking care of each other.

At break, she went to Michael's classroom. Miss McDrane was sitting at her high desk, correcting papers. Outside, Charlie was lying in the sun. Aware of Carrie through the window, although it was closed (on such a day!), he sat up and lifted his tufted ears. She frowned and shook her head – *not now, Charlie* – and stood before the teacher's desk, putting her hair behind her ears to show a serious, responsible face, still scarred, and with a slightly bloodshot eye.

'What do you want? I'm busy.' Miss McDrane was not correcting papers. She was reading a letter on blue airmail paper with an Australian stamp. From a man who had gone all the way to the bottom of the world to get away from her?

'It's about Michael. My brother.' Although the school was not very large, you could not be sure that people like Miss McDrane knew who you were.

'What about him? He's dropping down. Not that he was ever up, in my opinion. He's neglected. It's not right, the way you children live, like gipsies, on your own.'

'My mother is there.' Mother had stayed on for a while after Carrie was better.

'Is she?' Miss McDrane raised an eyebrow like a furry caterpillar.

'I don't tell lies,' Carrie lied.

'I didn't say you did, my dear girl. Why are you so touchy?'

'Because you don't seem to trust us.' (And I am not your dear girl.) 'If you don't believe my mother is at home, why don't you come and see for yourself?'

'Well, I—' The last, and only time Mother had met Miss McSewer, she had sent her packing with a flea in her ear.

'Come to tea at the weekend. She'd love to see you.' Now that *was* a lie.

'I'd be delighted.' So was that.

There was no telephone at World's End. Before the end of the week, Arthur, the boy who helped the old lady in the sweet shop post-office, sped down the lane on his sleek racing-bicycle, which was like a greyhound compared to lumbering Old Red. He banged the horseshoe knocker as hard as he could, although several people were outside the house, and he could see them.

'No need to knock the house down.' Mother got up from the flower bed where she was planting some nasturtiums and china-blue asters to see them through the summer.

'Urgent telegram.'

'How do you know it's urgent?' Everyone knew that Arthur read everything that came in and out of the post-office. Bessie Munce, the postmistress, steamed open letters over the kettle in her back parlour, and read all the postcards from people on holiday. Sometimes they added a message at the bottom of the card: 'Hullo, Bessie', because they knew she would see it.

'Because it says, "Urgent and confidential. Report for duty at once".' Arthur knew that everyone knew he knew. If Bessie Munce sealed down the telegram envelope with her mauve tongue, Arthur would stop on the way and work it open with a special paper knife he carried for the purpose.

'It's from Dad!'

Mother's shout brought everybody running. Carrie from the stable. Michael from up a tree. Em from the hammock, with a book and a kitten. Any communication from their father was a rare and wonderful event.

' "URGENT AND CONFIDENTIAL." ' Mother read it out, her hands earthy, her slacks torn at the knee, grass and twigs in her hair. She could not do gardening, or anything else, without getting in a mess.

' "URGENT AND CONFIDENTIAL. THE LADY ALICE IS READY TO SAIL ON A SHORT TRIAL CRUISE STOP CREW IS ORDERED TO REPORT FOR DUTY AT ONCE STOP WITH LOVE FROM THE CAPTAIN." '

'I'd like to show him how to write a telegram,' Arthur said. 'He doesn't want to waste money putting in all those extra words.'

'Money is no object.' Em gave him one of her looks, with a monkey jaw and narrowed blue eyes.

'I'll have to go.' Mother looked round at them, half pleased at being needed on the boat, half worried about being needed here too. 'Do you mind, my dears?'

'Of course not.' Carrie had not told her yet about Miss

McDrane, because it would have spoiled her week, fussing and worrying and saying, 'I wish we didn't have to have that woman to tea – will she expect cake?'

Arthur looked from one to the other of the family, his ears pricked to be able to report the conversation back to Bessie Munce at headquarters.

'Want me to draft you out a reply?' He whipped a pad of telegram forms out of his jacket pocket, took a pencil from behind his ear and licked the point. He was a sharp boy, who would go far in the post-office.

While he was composing a message for Mother, Michael took Carrie behind the corner of the house.

'Shouldn't we tell her about Miss McDrane coming to tea?' he asked, too loud.

'No.' Carrie put her hand over his mouth and pulled him into the ivy at the angle of the chimney. 'Because then she might not go. She doesn't really want to anyway.'

'She told Dad she did. Your hand smells of horse.'

'Lucky you. They don't always mean what they say, you know.'

'Mm.' Michael considered that. 'Would marriage be easier if they did, or more difficult?'

'I don't know. We might find out one day.'

'Would you marry me, Carrie?' Michael proposed charmingly.

'Any day.'

'Before Sunday? *That* would give Miss McGutter something to run down her drainpipe. What are we going to do? If she finds us here alone, she might send down the Nutshell again, and then we're sunk.'

The Nutshell was a Social Worker called Miss Nuttishall, who had once threatened – as grown-ups sometimes do when they see a good thing going – to put a stop to their wonderful life, alone here with the animals.

'We'll ask Mrs Figg to come.' Mrs Figg, Lester's mother, had helped them before, cleaning up the house before the Dreaded Nutshell came. They would have her at World's End on Sunday, motherly in her rose-patterned overall at the stove, broad in the beam, flour to the elbows; Carrie could see it now, even smell the baking scones.

Thirteen

Their mother left them that evening after Tom came home, waving out of the back window of Mr Peasly's loose-sprung taxi, her bell of fair hair bouncing over the ruts.

Lester went for a ride on Peter. Carrie was sitting in the high open doorway of the hay loft over the barn, waiting for him to come back, her eyes closed against the evening sun, when she heard a car stop in the lane.

She stood up and looked down. It was Mrs Figg's little blue car with a plastic flower on top of the aerial. Carrie went down the loft steps, through the ancient litter and dust and mealy smells of the barn, and out to the car.

Mrs Figg had a girl with her. It was Liza, the girl at Mount Pleasant, who had climbed over the wall and held John while Carrie talked to Lester in the boiler room of the greenhouse.

'Hullo.' She grinned sourly at Carrie. She was wearing a skirt. Her dark red hair was brushed back. She had a lot of pale lipstick and an enormous amount of eye make-up.

'Where are you going?' Carrie bent her knees to talk through the window of the small car. 'To a party?'

'It's to annoy my mum.' Liza blinked her loaded lashes at Carrie. 'She says I make myself look cheap.'

'Now that's enough, Liza. You know your mother thinks the world of you,' Mrs Figg said comfortably. 'Liza is going home,' she told Carrie.

'Oh – I'm glad.'

Liza made a face.

'We're early for the train, so I thought I'd drive by and

pick up that boy of mine,' Mrs Figg said. She didn't have to ask, 'Is he here?' He almost always was.

She and Liza sat on the rickety bench outside the house, where the old men had once sat and talked country gossip over mugs of beer in the old days when this was Wood's End Inn. Carrie tried to think of the right way to ask Mrs Figg about tea on Sunday.

Tom came out and sat on the grass near Liza. He talked about his job with the vet, and about some of the things he and Alec Harvey had done.

He used to say, 'Mr Harvey repaired a fractured femur', or, 'Mr Harvey spotted the trouble and saved the cat.' Now it was, 'Mr Harvey and I had to operate', or, 'Mr Harvey and I gave the old dog a few more years of life.'

'I've got an old dog at home,' Liza said. 'He's the only reason I want to go back.'

'Oh come along now Liza,' began Mrs Figg in her comfortable, Mount Pleasant matron voice. 'You know that's—'

But Liza paid no attention. 'Can you imagine anyone who likes Mount Putrid better than home?' she asked Tom. 'That's what mine's like.'

'I'm sorry,' Tom said. He sat with his long arms round his bony knees. He and Liza looked at each other sadly.

Cantering along the grass verge of the road, like a loose-sitting cowboy in a Western film, came . . .

'What is that?' Mrs Figg stood up.

'It's Lester. Your son,' Carrie added helpfully.

'But what's that thing he's riding?'

'A horse.'

'I can see that, dear,' Mrs Figg said patiently, as if Carrie were an especially stupid Mount Pleasant girl. 'Where did he get it?

'He's part Arab, part thoroughbred, part New Forest, the most beautiful action you—'

'I said, where did he get it?'

'It was given to us.'

'Don't try me, Carrie. I've had a hard day at work.'

Lester hopped Peter over the shallow dry ditch and came towards them over the lawn. What with Henry and Lucy and the dabbling ducks, and Oliver getting out of the meadow, or drawing the bolt of his loose box, the lawn was a disaster anyway. But daisies came up all over it, and tufts of tiny yellow flowers, like microscopic stars.

'That's a nice horse, son.' Mrs Figg folded her strong arms and pursed her mouth and nodded horsily, although she knew nothing about horses.

'The best.' Peter put his head down to the grass and Lester slid down to the ground over his tail.

'Where did you get him?'

'Well, once upon a time, there was this man called Mr No Thanks. And he had this evil daughter, you see . . .' Lester began to tell the adventure, telling it well, acting it out, putting on different voices, making a good story out of it, to entertain his mother and Liza.

Liza was entertained. Her eyes lit up behind the defiantly heavy make-up. Her pale mouth lifted at the corners.

Mrs Figg was not entertained. When Lester had finished with the scene in which Mr Novak had said he'd be glad if they kept the horse, she said in a voice that was quiet, but loaded, 'I thought you promised me you'd make up no more tales.' Many of the things that Lester told her were too fantastic for her to believe.

'It's true.' He looked surprised. He had not thought of her doubting this story.

'What would you do with such a boy?' Mrs Figg turned in exasperation to Tom, who was nearest in age to being on her side. 'He must think I'm soft in the head, the tales he spins. Talked to a spider . . . Saw a city at the bottom of the pond . . . Rich man gives him a valuable horse . . . I don't know what's to become of him, I swear.'

'It is true though,' Tom said. 'Mr Novak did—'

'You're all in league against reason.' Mrs Figg threw up her hands. 'Come along Liza, or we'll miss that train.'

'I hope we bloomin' do,' Liza said sulkily.

'When I was a girl, we didn't talk to our elders like that. I don't know what young people are coming to.' Mrs Figg was quite huffed. 'You come along home with me, young Lester Figg,' she said.

'I'll just put Peter away.' Lester stood astride Peter's bent neck, and the horse lifted his head and slid him down on to his back.

'You'll do no such thing.' His mother caught his bare leg and pulled him off again. 'Carrie can take the horse. You're coming home with me and tidy your room. It looks like a battlefield. And if you don't get rid of those caterpillars before your dad gets home . . .'

She grumbled him away. Carrie ran after them. 'Could you come to tea on Sunday, Mrs Figg?' No time to explain.

'I'll be busy.'

'Couldn't you—'

'I'm sorry.'

She got Lester and Liza into the car. Tom and Carrie stood at the edge of the ditch and watched them drive away. Liza's white face looked back wistfully. Lester was on the floor.

Fourteen

There was no time to worry about what would happen on Sunday if Miss McDrane found no motherly woman at World's End.

Joey, the black woolly monkey, was in trouble. Bad trouble.

Not that trouble was a new thing with him. He was supposed to be in his big cage if there was no one with him. But everyone hated to see him in there, and everyone was always taking him out.

And then forgetting him.

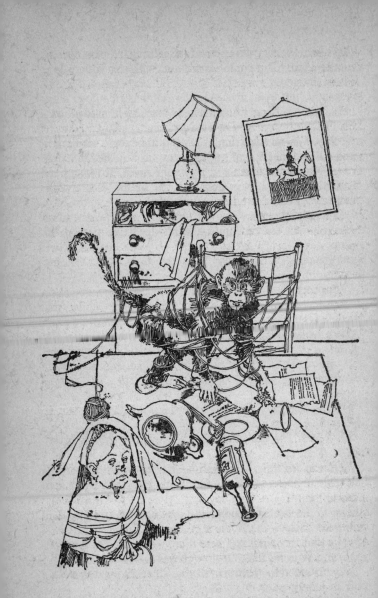

Joey, the black woolly monkey, was in trouble . . .

By the time they remembered, or came back from school, or woke in the morning, the room would look as if a horde of desperadoes had rampaged through it, searching for buried treasure.

Books hurled from the bookcase. Pages torn out and scattered all over the floor. Em's knitting wool wound in a maze round table legs and chairs. Michael's invention for draining spaghetti smashed into matchsticks on the kitchen flagstones. Drawers open and ransacked. Towels draped on the pictures and over the cracked bust of Queen Victoria without a nose, which Lester had found at the dump and brought as an Easter present. Cup handles broken off and stuffed down the sink. Saucers slid under the dresser. Joey himself swinging in Carrie's bridle which hung on a door knob, black eyes gleaming from a face plastered white with scouring powder.

'Sometimes I wonder,' Mother had said, snatching away an aspirin bottle, which Joey had found in the bathroom, 'whether this darling creature is a suitable pet for you.'

'He's not our pet,' Carrie said. 'He's our friend.'

'Well ...' Mother could not deny that, since it was she who had taught them, years ago, to treat animals as equals, not possessions. 'But it's the wrong kind of life for a jungle animal.'

'But it's a life. He'd have died in the awful pet shop. And if he'd gone for research—'

'He'll die if he eats all the aspirin, you can tell him from me.'

Medicine bottles of any kind were Joey's passion. When Mrs Figg had been sitting outside the house, she had put her handbag on the ground. Joey had opened it while she was talking to Lester, and found the bottle of slimming pills, which she carried about like a good luck charm, but never actually took, because they were supposed to take away your appetite, and being slim wasn't worth that.

They found Joey next morning in his chair by the stove, with the empty bottle in his limp hand.

'Dead!' shrieked Michael, who had come down first.

71

Carrie came running. 'He's passed out.'

They wrapped him in a rug, and Em ran down the lane to get Mr Peasly's taxi. He rushed them through the country roads, leaning hard over, like a racing driver, to corner on two screaming wheels. Carrie had been slapping Joey to keep him awake. In the taxi, Mr Peasly's driving did it for her.

Alec Harvey, the vet, was a cheerful young man who was not surprised at anything that came through his surgery door. Local children brought him frogs and fish and birds with broken wings. If they couldn't pay, he helped them anyway. A mother from the new housing estate, which was called Newtown, had brought her screaming baby once, because the doctor wouldn't come and she couldn't get to the hospital. Alec Harvey had taken a green and white marble out of the baby's ear. He had it displayed in a jar on a shelf, and had stuck a medicine bottle label on the frame of his vet's certificate: 'Also Baby Doctor.'

'A monkey on slimming pills.' He scratched his curly brown head. 'They didn't teach us *that* in college.'

He and Tom gave Joey a double dose of ipecacuana, to make him throw up the pills. Nothing happened, except that Joey looked more uncomfortable than before, and began to cry a little, rounding his mouth to say, 'Oh, oh, oh,' in Carrie's lap.

'Now listen here, you beggar,' Mr Harvey said through clenched teeth. 'You're not going to die.' He gave him another dose, and took him away from Carrie just in time.

Mr Harvey was very pleased. 'Also Monkey Doctor' he wrote on a label, and stuck it on the frame of his Certificate of Veterinary Medicine.

Mr Peasly, who felt that he had saved a life by his two-wheel driving, was so pleased that he drove Carrie and Em and Michael to school for no extra charge.

'Why are you late?' The Headmistress, Mrs Loomis, met them in the corridor.

'Our monkey took an overdose of slimming pills.'

'Next time you invent an excuse, do make it a good one will you, people?'

She wasn't a bad old soul. 'They'll have to retire her soon,' Em said, as Mrs Loomis pottered away. 'She's getting soft.'

After school, they drove John back to Newtown to collect Joey. They took the torn and grubby pink blanket which had been the monkey's best possession ever since he came to live with them. He carried it about, fought with it, trailed it like a wing as he leaped among the high rafters of the barn, draped it over his ears for safety like an ostrich burying its head in the sand, and slept every night with a corner of the blanket in his mouth.

At the vet's, they found him climbing on the wire of one of the dog runs. He snatched the blanket, and ran to the wire roof and hung there by a foot and a tail, hugging the blanket, crooning to it, rubbing it over his black snub face.

'He's gladder to see that than he is to see us,' Carrie said. 'It's as bad as Mike with that old voodoo doll.'

Michael had had the hideous doll ever since a crabby neighbour had brought it the week he was born, and been offended because he was too young to look at it. He had eaten off its toes and fingers and pulled out its eyes and hair.

'When Miss McDrane found it in my satchel,' he said, 'she said I had a sick mind.'

Carrie groaned. 'Why did you have to remind me of *her*? It's only two days till Sunday.'

'So it is,' said Alec Harvey. 'Let's go for a ride.' He exercised a thoroughbred for a friend.

'Oh good. Can we race?' John could keep up for a quarter of a mile before the bay thoroughbred drew ahead like a galloping machine.

'*Oh*, no you don't, Carrie.' They were in the surgery now, and Em was tidying up, rearranging bottles with a pursed, finicky mouth, like Lester's mother when she attacked the crusted stove at World's End. 'You asked McSewer. We've got someone coming to tea,' she told the vet.

'Tea parties. Aren't you social?' He was washing his

hands. It was getting dark outside. As he straightened up and reached for the towel, he looked at the window, stared, then shook his head. 'Funny. I thought I . . .' He went to the door and looked out. There was no one there. But a wolf-hound in the kennels had begun to give voice, a long sad, howling noise which the other dogs took up in various sizes of yaps and howls and barking.

'Qui-utt!' Tom yelled down the passage like Miss McDrane trying to control her class. 'You want me to come out there?'

The dogs might have answered, 'Yes,' since they loved Tom. Some of the barking stopped, but the wolfhound went on.

'There *is* someone there.' Tom went out. They heard him walk round on the gravel, then he called to somebody and they heard him talking. Then a girl's voice. The side door to the waiting-room opened. Tom came in with the girl from Mount Pleasant. Liza, the girl with the long dark red hair who Mrs Figg had put on to the train to go home.

She looked tired and dirty and rumpled, as if she had been sleeping out of doors. In her arms she held an old dog, its hair in lumps, one eye clouded over, limp legs dangling.

Without asking any questions, the vet held out his arms and took the dog into the surgery and laid it on the shiny white table. It lay quietly, shivering and panting feebly.

'He's ill.' The girl put her hands to her hair, twisted it into a rope and let it fall round her tired face again. She wore an old pair of shorts, cut ragged at the knee, a sagging jersey, dirty bare feet. She did not look at all like the girl who had sat in Mrs Figg's car with her skirt and her thick make-up 'to annoy my mum'.

'I thought you lived in London,' Tom said. 'Why did you bring him here?'

Liza looked round the room warily, as if she expected to be caught and slapped back into Mount Pleasant. 'You talked about the vet.' She nodded at Mr Harvey. 'I thought he would help.'

'I'd like to.' He had been examining the dog. 'But the old

74

fellow is pretty far gone. Why don't you leave him here and I'll see what I—'

'You're not going to put him to sleep?' Liza clutched at the dog's matted coat so fiercely that he whimpered.

'I hope not. Sometimes it's the kindest thing. But not without asking you, of course.'

'No!' Liza set her jaw so as not to cry. She was trembling too, like the dog.

Carrie gave Joey and his blanket to Michael, and went to Liza. Tom put his hand on her arm. But before they could comfort her, a terrible din and commotion started up in the waiting-room as four small boys burst in, wild-eyed and shouting, with a cat that had a fish hook caught in its mouth.

'He went to get the bait and he—'

'On the hook—'

'Poor old Tom, his old mouth—'

'Bit of cod, it was. My Auntie give it us—'

'Laid it down on the bank and he sneaks up—'

'Always loved a bit of cod—'

'Oh, the blood—'

They all talked at once.

Liza picked up her dog. The cat was laid on the operating-table, and Carrie held it while Tom quickly shaved a place on its leg to inject anaesthetic, and Mr Harvey snipped the end of the hook and pulled it out with forceps without drawing back the barb. He put two stitches in the torn lip and when the cat came round and the commotion was settling, they realized that Liza had slipped out, and taken her dog.

Tom went outside to look for her, but she had gone.

Fifteen

A man who bred racing whippets had paid his bill at last, so Alec Harvey, whose pockets always burned when they had money in them, took Tom and Carrie and Em and Michael out for supper. They lit the paraffin lamps on the two-wheeled trap, and John waited outside the fish-and-chip shop quite contentedly, since people who came out gave him some of their chips.

One man's chips he wouldn't eat. 'Go on you beggar.' The man was insulted. 'What's the matter with this nag?'

Carrie took the potato and tasted it. 'He won't eat them without salt.'

'Bad luck on him then,' said the man, 'because the doctor has dared me to eat salt, else my legs will go up like balloons.'

They dropped Mr Harvey at home, and drove away from the crowded, lit Estates and down the dark road at the edge of the hills, licking their fingers and singing.

They sang very loudly as they approached a particular corner with a lone tree and a dark swampy thicket that smelled rank and rotten.

> '*And then the MAN, quite ill at EASE,*
> *Said, "Brrring some brrread sir, if you plee-hee-hease!"* '

The corner was unpleasant in the daytime. At night, it was scary, even with Tom. Years and years ago, said the legend hereabouts, a girl had eloped with her lover, the two of them riding on a white horse. But the girl's maid had betrayed her, and the father was waiting in the lone tree with a noose of rope. As they rode below, he slipped the rope over the young man's neck and jerked him off the horse. He hung there, choking to death, while the girl and the terrified horse

76

plunged into the swamp, sinking deeper and deeper into the sucking bog until they were drowned.

And still, it was said, on the right kind of night, you might see the vague shape of the young man swinging from that high branch (or was it just the shadow of a cloud across the moon?) and hear the despairing cries of the girl as she sank helpless into the swamp (or was it just the wind in the line of poplars?).

The corner was called 'Hard-to-come-by', even on the maps, because horses had never liked to go past it. Sure enough, as they neared the line of poplars and the lone tree, John slowed to a walk, peered, and dragged the trap to the other side of the road.

'You see.' Carrie shivered. Was it better to look at the tree and the swamp, or not to look? 'He does know something.'

'*You* do,' Tom said. 'You send him the thought through the reins.'

'No. *He* sends the thought back to *me*. Like when you're jumping, you can tell if a horse is going to refuse.'

'You've got it wrong.' Tom could argue all night once he got started. 'He can tell if you're scared of a jump, and that's why he refuses.'

'But I'm only scared because I get the message from him that he doesn't like the look of it.' Carrie could argue too.

They argued into a patch of damp mist. Trees and hedges retreated into vapour like a mountain top into clouds. The yellow light of the lamps did not reach the road. John's long ears were edged with an eerie luminous sheen. He shied again.

'You see,' Tom said, 'you've made him spooky.' But John had swerved to avoid someone in the road. A girl carrying something in her arms. Liza was trudging along in the dark mist with her old dog.

Carrie said, 'Ho!' sharply. She had taught John to stop without the bit, like they did in Western films.

'Where are you going?' Tom jumped down.

'Dunno.' In the wavering light of the lamp, Liza's face

77

was full of shadows, her damp hair hanging over the dog like a shawl.

'Come back with us.' Tom handed the dog up into Em's lap. He pushed Liza up too, and trotted home beside the trap with his hand on the shaft, matching John's hoof-beats.

Approaching the edge of their wood where the road ran through the tunnel of beeches was like coming into the home stretch. John leaned into the collar and quickened his jog. But at the crossroads with the hollow tree and the letter box in the wall where no one ever posted letters and no postman ever took them out, he stopped, peered, and let out some dragon snorts, to frighten an enemy, or give himself courage.

What on earth? There was nothing there but the hollow tree and the wall and the letter box and the heap of stones the roadmenders had left.

The mist had cleared, but there was no moon, and the dark was settling down thick and early. Beyond the flickering light of the oil lamps on the front of the trap ('I'll have you prosecuted,' the village policeman swore, 'if you take that contraption out on the roads at night'), the heap of stones moved. A man who had been sitting there got up, and as he moved away under the hedge to the side road, he looked at them.

The thick black hair and beard, the leering, gap-toothed mouth. The huge gun on one shoulder. A wretched skeleton of a dog dragging behind him on a piece of rope.

'*Black Bernie!*' Carrie whispered. She had not seen him since she and Lester had kidnapped first Perpetua and her puppy and then John from his horrid clutches. 'What's he doing here?'

'Looking for something to shoot.' Tom took John's bridle and led him across the road and into the familiar wood, which encased them like a warm bath. 'He's a night person. He hunts at night.'

'He's a vampire,' Michael said chattily. He had been dozing before, but he always became lively when he got near home and bed. 'We'll bury him at the crossroads with a stake through his heart.'

'And garlic on his breath.' Carrie would never forget the poisonous reek of Black Bernie threatening her from the doorway of his filthy stinking hovel. 'He couldn't possibly have recognized John, could he?'

'Not a chance.' Tom slapped John's firm brown neck as he trotted beside him. 'He's a different horse from that wreck you brought home.'

'It couldn't be why he's hanging round here? Why he looked at us like that?'

'The evil eye,' Michael said, with relish. 'He's up to no good.'

'He's never up to any good,' Em said. 'So why worry? The day you see Black Bernie helping an old lady across the road or giving a child a sweet – that will be the day to start worrying.'

Lester was waiting for them at World's End. As they came out of the wood and swung round the corner of the blackthorn hedge, they saw lights in the windows. At the sound of John's hoofs, the front door let out a widening slot of light on to the path. Dogs and cats ran out, with Lester behind them, and finally the lumbering shape of Henry the ram, a rolling mass of wool on inadequate feet.

'How's Joey?' They had not seen Lester since Joey ate his mother's slimming pills, but somehow he knew. Like a jungle native communicating through a mysterious tele-graph of the Bush, he had his ways of knowing what was going on, even though he went to a different school in a different village.

They handed the monkey down to him, wrapped in the dog-haired rug which was the cover of the kitchen sofa, the first thing they had snatched up yesterday when they rushed him off to the vet. Liza got down, and held up her arms for Em to give her the old dog. He was very limp.

'Is he dead?' Lester peered, more interested in the dog than the surprise of seeing Liza, who he thought was in London.

She shook her head. 'But he would have been if I hadn't taken him away from there.'

'Where?'

'Where *she* lives.' Liza would not say 'Home', or 'My mother'. 'But don't tell your mum I'm on the loose,' she added quickly, 'or she might chuck me back in the cells.' Most of the girls were quite happy at Mount Pleasant, but they always talked of it as if it were a dungeon.

Tom took Liza into the house, and Lester went with Carrie to unharness John and feed him. Then they went into the kitchen, where Em had made tea, and everyone sat on the floor round the embers of the stove, because Liza, having found someone she could talk to, wanted to talk.

Sixteen

'. . . I'm not going to whine,' she said roughly. She talked very rough, very tough and embittered, sitting on the floor staring into the dying stove, with her arms round her knees. 'I tried whining when I was smaller, and it didn't get me nothing but a smack across the side of the head. "Bit deaf in one ear, this child," the doctor said. "Chronic." Yeah, I felt like saying, she's chronic, she is all right, my mum is.'

'She hit you?' Tom tried to sound casual, so Liza wouldn't think he had been nowhere and seen nothing.

'Too right she did, after my dad walked out. But I began to hit her back when I was bigger. Well, you have to, don't you?'

Everyone nodded, except Michael, who was asleep among Perpetua's new puppies, with his head buried in her soft speckled side.

'Because she never knocked Hubert about, see? That was the worst of it. That's why I – well, if you want to know why I got sent to Mount Putrid, it was because of Hubert, my rotten little brother. Everything's Hubert. Her little angel. Can't do no wrong, and so when he'd tell her things to get me in trouble, she'd believe him. All right, some of it was true. It *was* me did them pictures on the blackboards at school, and when the desks caught fire – well, least said . . . I done a few jobs, never took much, mostly cigarettes and stuff. Took a car once, me and a girl who was in this gang I went with. We drove to Clacton and it fell into a canal. Laugh! We thumbed a lift home and Hubert told me mum I'd run off with a sailor.'

Lester sat cross-legged, with his head on one side, alert, his dark bright eyes reading Liza's face. Em lay on her stomach with a scarf round her hair, frowning under it because she was thinking, not because she didn't like the story. Tom lay on his back smiling lazily, his long legs on the seat of a chair, long brown hands under his head, the striped cat Nobody going gently up and down on his chest as he breathed. Carrie sat with her elbows on her knees and her chin in her hands, staring at Liza in the lamp-light.

'What did she do to you?' she asked, enthralled.

'Played war. Took me out of school and put me to work in the shop. She has this lousy little shop, see, sells a few groceries and vegetables and fruit and that, near the council flat where we live. It's the only one, so she cheats the old age pensioners and the little kids who can't walk to the High Street. Gives them the rotten apples and spuds from the bottom of the pile and shorts them on the change. I told 'em, "Take the bag and help yourself", and when my mum came back from bingo and found them taking all the good tomatoes from the top, she yelled out they was pinching the stuff and she'd fetch the coppers. "And you can tell 'em Liza's been taking shillings from the till," pipes up old Hube, Mother's little angel, so I bashed him one and he fell into a bin of sprouts and I run off. I run – oh, I don't know – up the Midlands somewhere. I lived with these old tramps, on the road. One of them died. In a railway siding, it was. I sat in this cattle truck and held his old hand when he was dying and he says, "Liza, look after me dog," he says. Dusty, he called him, because he always was.'

She put out a hand to stroke the old dog's head. 'I took him back to our flat, because he needed food. My mum was wild. She only likes pedigree dogs, like this fat pug she's got. She was going to put me to work in a factory. Putting holes in the buttons. She wanted to cut my hair.'

She put her thumbs under her long tangled red hair and shook it behind her shoulders. Carrie did the same. She would never cut hers. She understood when Liza went on. 'She got out the scissors, so I run out and got in this car where they'd left the keys and drove away – right through the wall of a house where the people were watching telly. Their faces!'

Everyone laughed, and the love bird Gabby woke up and cackled, and ran his beak along the bars of his cage as if he were playing the harp.

'All right then, that's the story,' Liza said. 'Think what you like, I don't care.'

'Nor do we.' Tom spoke for them all.

Lester said, 'My mother never tells me anything about what the girls have done, so I imagined something much worse.'

'In court, they said I was beyond control.' Liza smiled to herself, remembering. 'The worst thing about being sent to Mount Putrid was leaving poor old Dusty. That stinker Hubert said he'd look after him – I might have known – but when I got home the other day, there was that bloated pug snoring in the armchair and Dusty, he – he – my poor old dog was out on the roof in a sort of leaky shed for a water tank. So I had to take him away.'

'Poor Liza,' Tom said, but she jumped up and cried, 'Don't give me none of your pity! It was my fault for leaving him there.'

'I think he's a bit better.' Dusty was on a pile of bran sacks in a warm corner out of the draught. Tom had given him a nip of brandy that Mr Mismo had brought to celebrate Christmas and anyone's birthday. When it was nobody's birthday, he invented one for an animal – 'Happy birthday, hamster', 'Many happies to a fine tortoise' – so he could drink their health. 'I'll get some stuff for him from Mr Harvey tomorrow. Vitamins. Something to get rid of the fluid on his chest. Pills for his heart. As a matter of fact, Liza, you look worse than the dog.'

When she jumped up, Liza had realized how dead beat she was. She had collapsed into a chair by the table, with her head on her arms. 'I walked . . . I didn't have nowhere to sleep . . .'

She was too nearly asleep already to get her upstairs. They put her on the sofa with a coat over her and left her there, with Michael and the puppies, and Gabby blacked out with a towel over his cage, and the old dog snoring and twitching on the pile of sacks.

Lester wanted to stay the night, but decided to go home to please his mother, so she might change her mind about coming to tea on Sunday. He got a lift from a boy on a motorbike, but he was still so late home that she was angry anyway and took a swipe at him with her dressing-gown cord. There were some people's mothers you just couldn't please.

Liza's was another. First she had been glad to shove her off to Mount Pleasant. Now she wanted to have her at home earning money.

'She'll set the coppers on me,' Liza was edgy and nervous. 'They'll make me go back.'

'They won't know where you are.'

'They'll find out. You'll see them creep up the lane. Big black car. I know 'em.'

'I'll set Charlie on them,' Michael said.

Charlie thumped his tail and yawned loudly with a sound like words. Michael had taught him to play dead by catching a moment when he wanted to flop down anyway. He was now teaching him to talk, by catching him at a moment when he was stretching his jaws to yawn loudly and then saying, 'Hullo', so that Charlie's yawn sounded like an answering 'Hu-yo'.

Michael had written this in his private book, *Micheal's Dog Lores*: 'A dog nead a lot of beath to tak so he youn.'

'There was this dog in Liverpool,' Liza said, 'used to go into a snack bar and say, "Gimme a ham roll." '

'How do you know?'

'I been there.' In all the strange stories she told, Liza had never just *heard* about it. She had always 'been there', whether she had or not.

Michael wrote in his book: 'A dog in Liverpol go into a sak bar and sad (gime a ham rol).'

Liza did not try to correct the spelling. She baked him a special loaf of sweet bread she had learned to make at Mount Pleasant, using all the currants Em was saving to make rock cakes for Miss McDrane's tea party on Sunday. Liza and Michael ate the whole loaf without even sitting down.

Em was furious. 'Who said she could move in here and use all our things? She took my shampoo.'

'Why can't you be nice?' Carrie kicked her. 'She's a refugee.'

'Shut up with that being nice!' Liza's quick proud temper had caught fire from Em's. 'I'm leaving.'

'Hooray,' Em said, but Carrie was having an idea. It was beginning to bubble up in her head like fruit salts.

'Please stay, Liza. We want you.'

'Shut up being nice, I said!'

'I'm not. But it's this woman at the school, she's coming here to make trouble about us being on our own. If there was someone here baking bread and stuff – an older girl—'

'Old girl. Old as God. Thanks very much. You just want to make use of me.'

'Look, you can't have it both ways,' Carrie said reasonably. 'You won't let us be *nice* to you, and you won't let us *use* you. What on earth *do* you want?'

Liza ran outside. They did not see her any more. When

Tom came home, he went out calling and searching the meadow and the farm buildings.

'Don't bother dragging the duck pond,' Em called through the window over the stove, where she was stirring 'Esmeralda's End-of-the-week Soup'. She was still angry about the shampoo and the currants. 'She'll be back to eat.'

But Liza was not back for supper. She was not back when they went to bed. They thought she had left the old dog in their care and gone for good.

In the middle of the night, Carrie was suddenly awake, not naturally, but as if something had woken her. She lay listening. No dogs barking. No hysterical alarms about foxes from the hen house. No sound from the horses. No clatter of Joey taking a night flight among the saucepans. No kitten crying in the top of a tree. She listened to the silence, only the poplar trees across the road endlessly turning their leaves inside out in the small breeze.

It was not her ears, but her nose that had woken her. Wafting up the staircase, curling under her door like aromatic smoke, the most delicious, crusty, hungering smell in the world.

She ran down in the old long shirt of Tom's that did for a nightdress. In the kitchen, in the light of a flickering row of candles on the shelf behind the stove, Liza was baking bread.

Miss McDrane arrived on Sunday, very polite in a shiny straw hat and white gloves, knocking on the door with the pearl handle of her best umbrella to show that she was not going to be put down by anybody's mother. And they were able to take her proudly through into the kitchen, where Liza, in a flowered apron hastily made by Em from one of the bedroom curtains ('Keep her out of that room!') was cutting home-made bread and setting the table for tea with Mrs Mismo's best matching teacups.

'My mother was *so* disappointed to miss your visit,' Carrie said in the sugary voice with which she camouflaged the one that came out rude for people like Miss McDrane. 'She had to go away, but our cousin Elizabeth is staying here to look after us.'

'Indeed.' Miss McDrane drew in her waist and stuck out her top and bottom. Her pink-rimmed guinea-pig eyes flicked round the room to find fault, but came back to the tea table. She took a paper handkerchief out of her sleeve and dabbed at the corners of her watering mouth. She was very greedy. At school lunch, where Mrs Loomis made teachers take tables 'to civilize the savages', nobody wanted to sit at Miss McDrane's table, because she short-served people to leave more for her, and when it was shepherd's pie or macaroni cheese, she kept the crusty bits round the edge for herself. She watched your piece of bread to see if you were going to eat it, and then pounced as soon as someone got up to clear plates, saying, 'Waste not, want not,' as she popped your bread into her mouth.

She managed to put away a lot of Liza's bread and cake, even while keeping both little fingers crooked high in the air to show she was a lady, and went away quite satisfied.

'I like a girl who can bake,' she said at the door, chasing the last crumbs of fruit cake round her mouth with her tongue. 'You don't find that these days.'

Drunk with food, she put up her umbrella although it wasn't raining, teetered to her car in her best shoes, and drove away, sitting bolt upright with her hat on straight, like Mrs Noah.

Liza collapsed on the doorstep, clutching Carrie. 'A girl who can bake!' she shrieked. 'If only she knew where I learned how! "*You don't find that these days.*" Too true, Miss McSmell. You only find it at Mount Putrid!'

Seventeen

When Carrie told Lester about the skeleton dog she had seen at the crossroads with Black Bernie, the adventure light came into his face and he began to make plans for rescue.

They were sitting in one of their special trees in the beech-wood, pretending to ride. The thick grey branches were shaped exactly like the neck of a horse. With a piece of rope for reins, you could sit in the crook of a branch against the trunk, and perform amazing feats like winning the Three Day Event at the Olympics, or crossing the Sahara on an Arab stallion.

With John and Peter in the meadow, they could ride any time they wanted to, but they still acted out this pretence, which they had invented before they ever had horses.

'We could hide in that hollow tree at night,' Lester suggested, 'and make a noise like ghosts. He'll let go the dog and run.'

'Don't forget he's got a gun.'

'People don't shoot at ghosts.'

'Black Bernie shoots at anything. He shoots at bottles in the dump. He shot the hat off Alan Tupper's scarecrow.'

'We could tell the police he hasn't got a dog licence.'

'How would we know?'

'I'll ask Arthur at the post-office.'

'We don't want anything to do with the police while Liza's here.'

'I can't just kidnap the dog,' Lester said, 'like I did Perpetua and Moses, because Bernie doesn't keep dogs in that outhouse anymore.'

'How do you know?'

'I spy round there from time to time, just to keep an eye on things.'

'When do you go?'

Lester looked vague, and stroked the neck of his tree horse. He didn't time his days like other people, and there seemed to be more hours in his.

'Why don't you take *me*?'

'This evening?'

When the sun was going down, Carrie saddled John, and Lester put a halter on Peter, and they rode across country to the small corner of hell where Black Bernie lived.

It was called Bottle Dump, because that was what it had been for as long as anyone could remember, a place where people chucked things they didn't want, and Black Bernie had chucked himself down there, which was very fitting.

It was a disused quarry below the gorse common, its steep sandy sides now overgrown with bushes and rank weeds, at one end the treacherous sheered-off edge where the Headless Horseman was still said to be seen, galloping to his death.

Carrie and Lester cut across a corner of the common, the horses hopping low gorse bushes like cats, and skirted the lip of the quarry, looking down into Bottle Dump over the leaning fence which the Headless Horseman had jumped.

I hate the dreadful hollow behind the little wood ...

The Tennyson poem might have been written here.

Its lips in the field above are dabbled with blood-red heath,
The red-ribbed hedges drip with a silent horror of blood,
And echo there, whatever is asked her, answers 'Death'.

Below them, the patched tin roofs of Black Bernie's shacks tilted crazily, the chimneys made of bent rusty drainpipes, the walls leaning against mounds of rubbish and old iron. Beyond, driven or towed or pushed into the bushes, or simply dropped over the edge of the quarry, a battered car with shattered glass lay with four wheels in the air like a dead beetle.

88

Carrie and Lester rode down the side of the hill into a clump of trees where they were hidden from Bottle Dump. Carrie had a halter over her bridle, and they tied up John and Peter and crept on all fours through the bushes until they could see the shacks.

A battered, bulky old car was outside the largest one, standing all askew on soft tyres, its dented boot half open, tied down with wire, so rusty and dilapidated that it looked ready to join the abandoned hulk on its back among the wretched refuse.

'*The Poacher!*' Lester whispered. He knew everybody's car.

The Poacher was a little mean man in clothes that were too big for him, useful, like a shoplifter's loose overcoat, for storage. He could sometimes be seen on the edge of the market, selling a few chickens and ducks. Always ordinary breeds of chickens and ducks, with no special markings. No way of telling if they were stolen. He lived in a home-made caravan, never long in the same spot. His laundry line was hung with rabbit skins. The rust stains on his car looked like old blood.

It was a warm evening, and the door of the shack stood open. From inside came a horrible sound, like the souls of lost cats in hell. Lester and Carrie crept closer and flattened themselves to the ground below a heap of stones. The Poacher and Black Bernie were singing.

Bernie came to the door with a wine bottle in his beefy hand, took a great gurgling swig and hurled the bottle at one of the rubbish piles, missing Lester and Carrie by inches.

'*Don't shoo-hoot the vicar—*' he sang, bellowing into the night.

'*The carving knife is quicker!*' The Poacher's howl was high and strident, as if he had a clothes peg on his nose. 'Come back in and open this other bottle, rot and damn your black soul. Me teeth are too far gone to bite off the neck.'

There was no sign of the skeleton dog. But when Carrie shifted slightly, dislodging a stone, another dog, a brown

*A battered, bulky old car was outside, and beside it stood
the Poacher and Black Bernie*

and white collie, crawled out of a tipped-over rain barrel and barked, throwing itself the length of its chain, and choking.

'Shut up, you devil!' Black Bernie aimed a kick at it, but was too drunk to reach. The dog went on barking hoarsely. Carrie and Lester were slithering quickly backwards towards the thicker shelter of the trees.

A gunshot cracked the air above their heads. 'There, you brute!' Bernie shouted at the dog. 'The next one will be for you.'

At the sound of the shot, Peter had pulled back and broken his halter rope. He had started for home, but luckily met a patch of sweet clover and stopped. He let Lester catch him easily – it had once taken Carrie and Tom and Mr Mismo (panting) two hours to get hold of him in the meadow – and Lester took off his belt to replace the broken rope.

They rode in silence for a while. Then Lester sighed and said, 'Did you see?'

'The dog,' Carrie said. 'It was somebody's pet. Well fed, healthy.'

'And the wine,' Lester said. 'He's come into some money. Something bad is up at Bottle Dump.'

And echo there, whatever is asked her, answers 'Death'.

Eighteen

After the tea party Liza disappeared for a couple of days, leaving the dog and a note that said she had gone 'to do a job'.

Burglary? There seemed to be nothing this girl would stop at; but when she came back, she had been to do a real job, hitch-hiking to the north country to help a friend from her old gang who had just come out of the hospital.

She arrived back in the RSPCA van. The Cruelty Man had met her on the road and given her a lift to World's End. 'I was coming anyway,' he told Carrie, 'to see if you've got any new dogs here.'

'Only Perpetua's puppies. Come and see them.' He spent a large part of his days at the kennel for lost and unwanted dogs and cats, but he was always ready to see a few more.

'The thing is,' he said, kneeling to stroke Perpetua's bony head, and praise her, 'I thought perhaps a dog might have – well, strayed here, the way animals do find their way to this place.'

'If we'd had any luck,' Carrie said, 'there might be a poor thin dog here like the skeleton of a ghost, that we wanted to rescue the other day.'

'I thought you kids weren't going to pinch any more animals.' The Cruelty Man tried to look severe, but his face wasn't made for it.

'Oh, we haven't,' Carrie said, although she wished they had. Where was that wretched dog now?

'Well, someone has.' The Cruelty Man stood up and brushed straw from the knees of his blue uniform. 'There's a big dog gone from a farmer near my place. And a lady rang me up this morning to say her dog had simply disappeared. Never runs off, but it's been gone four days. And Pine Tree Kennels, they lost two last week before they put padlocks on the runs.'

'What sort of dogs?'

'Two setters. Nice ones. The lady's was a sort of collie cross, it sounded like, though she didn't know how to describe it. Silky fur, pretty white face, plumy tail – you know how they carry on. They never say mongrel.'

'Why would anyone steal a dog, unless it's valuable?'

'I hate to tell you, Carrie.' The Cruelty Man looked at her sadly, the smile crinkles round his mouth and eyes straightened out into white lines in his tanned face. 'They're short of research dogs at the University. Especially biggish ones. They're paying good money for them, and some of the dealers – well, they don't ask where they come from.'

'Come with me,' Carrie said.

They drove to Bottle Dump. Black Bernie knew Carrie, and the Cruelty Man's uniform would make him suspicious, so they took Liza. They hid in the back of the van while she went boldly up to the shack with the excuse of asking the way.

'I'll put on a foreign accent,' she said, 'so he'll think I'm a lost stranger.'

They heard her knocking on the door, and shouting, 'Plees mister! I am lost girl, 'oo need 'elp from ze kind Eeng-leeshman!'

No roar from Black Bernie. No barking.

'Nobody home.' Liza came back to the van. While she watched the road, Carrie and the Cruelty Man searched round the shacks and dumps, but there was no sign of the brown and white collie. Where was it? Even the barrel and chain were gone.

That evening, Liza and Em went unhopefully into the larder to see what they could cook for supper. There wasn't much. A lot of their food money had gone to buy some more chickens. They could sell eggs to people who like to get them from hens that were running free, not caged like crimi-nals.

'Got to spend money to make money' was a good business motto, but it would be some time before they would make any money out of the new Rhode Island Red hens, Rosie, Redruth, and Rubella. They sat funkily under a gooseberry bush, like new girls at school and would not lay, while Dianne and Currier and their five conceited daughters patrolled with their feet picked up high, and dared them to come out.

Michael had sold some of his home-made stools at the church fête, but one of them had come back after it col-lapsed under a stout lady and she fell into the grate. Michael would have to sell another stool to pay her back her money.

Or sell some more stable manure to the fertilizer-hungry gardeners at the housing estates. But Carrie would not let him drive John in the muck cart with the sign he had written on the back: 'FINE FARM FERTILER. WE DELVER.' He was trying to build a small cart for Oliver Twist out of a wheelbarrow body and old pram wheels, but when he tried it out, Oliver trotted off with the broomstick shafts, the axle collapsed, and Michael was left sitting on the ground in the barrow.

Carrie should have driven the fertilizer over to the housing estates herself, but when they came back from school, John was tired . . . No, he wasn't, but it was more fun to ride him with Lester than to drive him in the muck cart . . .

'So you see,' Em told Liza, 'there's only a few odd bits of this and that—'

Liza poked about the slate shelves among the sad little saucers of left-overs, and said, 'I'll make Putrid Pie. That's what we had on Sundays at Mount P. Everything bunged into a pan and stirred up – different every time.'

She bunged and stirred, with the handle of a screwdriver, since she couldn't find a big spoon.

'Is that the chicken food?' Michael came into the kitchen.

'It's your supper,' Em said, 'so go and wash your hands.'

'What for?' He had not washed before meals since they lived with Aunt Val and she used to drag him shrieking to the basin.

'Do it,' Em said sternly. It was to get him turned away to the sink, so that he wouldn't see Liza bunging in the remains of Em's short crust pastry that no one would eat.

'What the eye don't see, the heart don't grieve over,' Liza muttered, rotating the screwdriver, and indeed, when they were all in the dining-room which used to be the saloon bar when World's End was an inn, everyone said the Putrid Pie was the best supper they had had for ages.

'Oh thanks very much,' Em said, huffed. But secretly, she was glad not to be stuck with all the cooking. Someone else's

94

food always tasted better, like sleeping in a bed you haven't made yourself.

Joey sat on the rung of Carrie's high stool at the bar, and she passed him down interesting snacks she found in the pie. She was feeling especially warm about him. Her worry about the dogs going to the research laboratories had taken her back to those dangerous days when she and Lester had saved Joey in the nick of time from the same fate.

That night, the little black monkey had indigestion. He rubbed his hairy stomach and groaned and rolled up his eyes like Charlie when he was playing dead.

'It's my fault,' Liza was filling a hot water bottle to comfort him. 'The Putrid Pie.'

'No, it's not.' Em came from the front of the house. 'He's been at the pills again.' She held out an empty bottle. 'Dusty's Digitalis. They were hidden in that blue jug on the mantelpiece, but *he* found them.'

When Carrie went to Mr Evans, the village chemist, to get some more pills for the old dog, she told him about the monkey.

'Aha!' he said. 'Monkey tricks, eh?' When you wanted something at the chemists, you had to wait through his feeble puns. 'You know what they say – more trouble than a wagonload of monkeys? Well, I'll fix his little wagon all right.' His rimless glasses glittered. He sucked his teeth and snickered at his own wit. Carrie waited with a face like a boot for him to get down to business.

He went down to the end of the counter where he mixed the medicines and stuck on labels with writing that no one could read.

'Did this once for a man who had a pet pig,' he told Carrie, while he fiddled about. 'Greedy as a pig, it was' (snicker, snicker). 'When there was nothing else to eat, it ate the wife's sleeping tablets and fell asleep by the side of the road. Got picked up for dead by the rubbish cart and woke up in a pile of garbage half a mile off the coast. All at sea, you might say. So I made up some capsules with pepper inside. Laugh! The man left 'em about, and when that pig got a taste of one,

95

he sneezed so hard he blew the ring right out of his nose. There you are, my dear.' He handed Carrie Dusty's tablets and a box labelled, 'Monkey Puzzle Pills'. 'That will be eighty pence and I thank you.'

'Will you put it on our bill?' Carrie asked faintly. She hated having to say that as much as shopkeepers hated having to hear it.

The capsules were a success. They put the box in the blue jug on the mantelpiece while Joey was watching with his ripe blackberry eyes, and then left him alone. Quite soon they heard a terrible racket. The sitting-room looked like an earthquake. Chairs were overturned, one curtain torn down, the poker stuck through the wastebasket, the tablecloth torn off and wrapped round the monkey, who was rolling about on the floor with streaming eyes, sneezing and sneezing.

'That's cruel,' Michael said.

'It's to save his life. He'll be all right in a – in a—' Carrie clapped her hand over her face and exploded through it like a volcano. Joey had scattered the pepper all over the room.

Nineteen

But the woolly monkey was not all right. He went on sneezing. Then he began to cough and wheeze. Instead of jumping about, always trying to be higher than everyone and throwing nutshells at your head, he walked like a crab, feebly sideways, or sat in a corner with his blanket over his head and his mouth stretched in a shape of woe.

'What's the matter?' Michael cuddled him. 'What's the matter, poor woollen monkey?' But Joey would only go, 'Oh . . . oh . . .'

'Monkeys only talk to each other,' Carrie said. 'They'd never let people know if they could talk, in case they were made to work and pay taxes.'

Because they thought it might still be the effects of the Monkey Puzzle Pills, they did not take him back to the vet for a while. But when they did, Mr Harvey took Joey's temperature, shot up his curly eyebrows and brought them down again in a worried frown.

'Hundred and four. Looks like pneumonia.'

'What can you do?' They looked at him; Carrie, Liza, Em and Michael, waiting.

'Don't look at me like that.' The young vet spread his hands helplessly. 'I'm not a monkey expert. It's easy for a doctor. He has only one kind of animal to learn about – people. A vet knows dogs and cats and horses and cows and pigs, but he can't know *everything*.'

'It says, "Also Monkey Doctor".' Michael pointed trustingly to the label Mr Harvey had stuck on his veterinary certificate.

'Oh Lord—' he swung away and reached for the telephone. 'There's a girl I know at the zoo over near Nettlefield. I'm going to ask her. Zoo hospital? Miss Lynch please ... Hullo – Jan? Alec Harvey. Look, I need your help.'

When he put down the telephone, he unbuttoned his white surgery jacket. 'She says bring the monkey to her at once. She'll find out what bug he's got, and put him in a special oxygen cage. I'll drive you. Tom, you hang on here. Take the temperatures and give the medicines. Check the stitches on that dog's leg. If anyone comes in, do first-aid, or whatever. Ask them to come back.'

They all got into his car, which had a wire screen across the back so that he could carry strange dogs without them jumping on to his neck while he was driving. He drove a car in the same way that he had ridden the bay thoroughbred in a point-to-point last spring: easily, casually, nipping in and out of the traffic as he had nipped through the field of tired horses to lead over the last fence and pound alone down the straight, with Tom, Lester, Carrie, Em and Michael screaming like maniacs at the winning-post.

A policeman pulled up beside him at a red light.

'What's the hurry then?'

'It's a matter of life and death!' Carrie poked her head out of the window.

'Going to the hospital?' The policeman saw the blanketed bundle on Liza's lap and thought it was a baby. 'OK. Good luck.'

The lights changed and Alec Harvey let the policeman pull ahead, so that he wouldn't see them turning, not to the people's hospital, but the zoo hospital.

In a building full of squeals and whistles and grunts and howls and growls and monkey chatter, they found Janet Lynch, with a stained white coat and very short hair and a blunt, square face. Her words were blunt and short too, never more than one syllable.

' 'Lo kids,' she greeted them. ' 'Lo Al. Let's see the monk.'

She checked Joey quickly and put him at once into a cage with a thick sealed glass door through which oxygen was piped in. He sat with his tattered blanket round his shoulders, blinking at Carrie and, as she watched him, already beginning to breathe better.

'Stay a bit,' Jan Lynch said, 'so he can see you. Here I'm short of help. You kids can feed the babes.'

She sat them on a bench at the other end of the room and brought small bottles of milk, and gave Em and Michael tiny monkeys, and Liza a lion cub, and Carrie a bear only a week old – animals whose mothers had died or wouldn't feed them.

'Pretty cosy,' Alec said. He was playing with two young chimpanzees in a child's play pen.

'Ought to come more,' Jan said. 'Vets should learn from zoos. Mad fad now to keep odd wild pets at home. See 'em on TV. "I want it!" Walk it on leash. Wear it round neck. Cubs in the kids' room. Snake in the back yard. Monk in the bed. Get sick in the end and no one knows what's up.'

'I'd like to learn,' Alec said, 'if I wasn't so busy. I wish my boy Tom could come for a while – these kids' brother. Be

98

useful to me if he could learn something here about exotic pets.'

'Wish he could, Al,' Jan said. 'Boy just left. I need help.'

'So do I,' Alec said.

'I'd work for you, Mr Harvey!' Carrie looked up eagerly from the baby bear. 'I could do everything that Tom does. I could ... Oh yes.' Her face dropped. 'I know. Don't say it. School. School, school, always rotten, stinking school. The best years of my life going to waste on algebra and the chief mineral products of Central Uganda.'

'I could work for you, Alec.' Liza stood up and put the little monkey back in its cage.

'I thought your mother wanted you at home.'

'I don't care.' She shook back her red hair and put on her lawless face. 'They can't make me.'

'They could send you back to Mount Pleasant,' Alec said, 'and that wouldn't be much help to me.'

'You mean, I *could* work for you?'

'If Jan wants Tom here, and he wants to come.'

'Lucky swine,' Carrie grumbled, holding up the little bear and patting his soft furry back to make him belch. 'Lucky Liza. Lucky Tom. Won't I ever be old enough to do *anything*?'

'I thought you wanted to stay being a child.' Em looked at her.

'I do. I want everything. I want – oh, I don't know what I want.'

'I want a towel,' Michael said. 'The milk has gone in one end of this monkey and right out the other.'

On the way home, Liza asked Carrie rather roughly, 'Is it – I mean, is it all right then, with you lot, if I—'

'Stay at World's End? We thought you were.'

They had got used to Liza. She was wild and unpredictable and noisy and clumsy, but they had got used to her, like a new animal.

Before they got home, she telephoned her mother's shop

99

from a call box, to say she wanted to stay at World's End and work for Alec Harvey. Through the glass, Carrie could hear the voice on the other end of the line, quacking like an infuriated duck, while Liza opened her mouth and waved her free hand and made fierce faces and couldn't get a word in edgeways.

She came out stamping her feet like Em when she was angry in boots, and tugging at her hair as if it was a bell rope.

'What did she say?'

'She's coming to see me.'

'What else?' The voice had quacked on for a full five minutes.

'Nothing else. She's coming.'

Twenty

Liza's mother came in a vulgar-looking purple van with

E. ZLOTKIN, GREENGROCER.
YOU WANT THE BEST? WE HAVE IT

painted on the side. She brought her son Hubert.

'Why did you have to bring that creep?' Liza asked aggressively.

'I knew you'd want to see dear little Hubert.'

'Only in hell,' Liza said boldly. She did not care what she said to anyone. Her mother's face swelled redder and her eyes bulged as if someone were blowing her up from inside. She was a loud, coarse woman, with a smell and a shine on her like bacon grease.

It was a very hot day when she came, one of the many of that glorious summer, with weeds and flowers and bramble vines running to jungle riot, and the horses and the donkey head to tail on the bare trampled ground under the wide chestnut tree, dedicating their days to the war of the flies.

Everyone was out at the back of the house, getting ready to give Liza's mother lunch out of doors. They had dragged out the old weather-scarred table and strapped a piece of wood to its broken leg, and glued a sardine tin under one of the others, to make all four more or less the same length. Em and Liza were laying out knives and forks and plates, stepping round or over Henry and Lucy and various puppies and cats who were hanging about to see what was going to happen. If eating was going to happen, they were going to be there. The goat was licking the sardine tin.

Michael was cutting grass with a collection of clacking old iron that he called a lawn-mower. He pulled it behind him with a strap round his chest, like a horse pulling a harrow. The dull blades clanked round, flattening the grass, if not cutting it.

Carrie was in the torn tennis net hammock reading, 'to improve her mind' for social conversation with Liza's mother. She was reading a library book called *Horses in my Life*.

'. . . And then there was the corky little bay who carried me for more years than I care to remember, sound in wind and limb and mild of eye . . .' It was fantastically dull, droning on like the bees in the potato flowers.

Carrie shut her eyes. She opened them with a start as the clack of the mower stopped and a great hullabaloo sounded from the front of the house. She rolled the hammock over to tip herself on to the ground, which was the fastest way of getting out, and ran round the house.

Liza was ahead of her, shouting, 'Put him down! Put him down, you rotten little beast!' Her brother Hubert had Dusty struggling in his arms, and yelling as if he had been run over.

Hubert dropped him awkwardly, and the old dog limped off through the hedge and into the wood, howling as if the devil was tied to his tail.

'Oh!' Liza stamped both her bare feet. 'Now look what you've done, you jerk!'

'I only went to pick him up. What have I done now?'

'You know he hates that. He's old and stiff and he's been ill—'

'I only wanted to pet him. Mum-may!' He ran to his mother like a great baby. 'She's just as mean as ever.'

Darling little Hubert was a blubbery overgrown boy of about eleven, with eyes like currants in dough and a wet pink baby mouth.

Liza's name was Jones. Her mother had gone back to her maiden name of Zlotkin when Mr Jones left her, which seemed a bad exchange for Jones. She sat at the table under the trees fanning herself with a plate, and stared at the animals as if they were wild beasts. Henry the ram, who had no tact, put his woolly head on her wide lap, and she pushed him off with her handbag and said, 'Get away, bad dog Charlie.'

'That's Charlie.' Michael politely pointed out the shaggy dog, spread out like a sheep's fleece under the shade of a bush.

'Twins, eh? Bit much, ain't it?'

Mrs Zlotkin was surprised to see Liza wearing the bedroom curtain apron and handing round the bread she had made. Not pleased. She was never pleased. But surprised. 'At least you learned something at that Mount Poison, or whatever they call it.'

'I can do more than you think,' Liza said. 'I got a job.'

'What sort of a job?' her mother asked suspiciously.

'With a vet.'

'A vet – what's all this?'

'An animal doctor. The Fieldings' brother works for him, but he's going to work at the zoo—'

'What for?' Mrs Zlotkin's eyes bulged like hard-boiled eggs.

'Because of the monkey.'

'What monkey?'

'Forget it.'

Liza had worked for two days cleaning houses in the village. Michael had washed a car, and Em had got extra money for baby-sitting 'above and beyond the call of duty' (getting bitten in the calf of the leg by Mrs Potter's middle brat), so it was a pretty good lunch. Hubert ate everything he could lay hands and teeth on, sighed and threw himself on the ground, denting the turf. He lay with his stomach sticking up, panting gently.

'It's not bad here.' It was the first time his mouth had been free to speak since the beginning of lunch.

'That's right, love.' His mother always agreed with him.

'So I can stay?' Liza pounced.

'I didn't say that. Minnie Boggs asked me to go to Clacton in their caravan. I'll need you at home to look after my little Hubert.'

'You want *me* to take care of *him*?'

'Kind Liza take care of poor Hubie.' He blinked up, laughing at her, his face pink and glistening from the juices of what he had put into it.

'I'll be—'

Liza was working herself up to explode with rage, but Mrs Zlotkin was having an idea, her face bursting with the effort. 'I might let him come here, though.' (No one had invited him.) 'Put roses in his cheeks, that would ' (They were crimson already with overeating.) 'All right, girl. If you want to stay, he comes too.'

'Always a snag to everything,' Liza muttered, and Em picked up a tray and grumbled into the kitchen, 'Hubert . . . Hube the Boob . . . What a summer.'

Carrie said nothing, torn between wanting Liza and not wanting dear little Hubie, so Michael put his brown, grubby fingers on the edge of the table and leaned forward as politely as a head waiter and said, 'Of course, Mrs Slotmachine, we'd love to have him.'

Mrs Zlotkin belched.

'Thanks for nothing.' Hubert lay on his back chewing grass, with Maud, the deaf white cat, on his stomach. He

103

picked her off all wrong, pulling a hind leg, and she squealed and struck out and ran up a tree.

'Mum-may!' He sat up and held out his podgy hand, trying to force tears. 'It scratched me!'

Squawking about blood poisoning, Mrs Zlotkin took him into the kitchen to wash the tiny scratch. Em was getting out cups of coffee, and Gabby was cackling from his cage, 'Cuppa tea cuppa tea cuppa tea', as he always did when he heard the rattle of china.

'Pretty Polly,' Hubert said. He stood on a chair to reach the cage, which hung from a ceiling hook that had once been used for curing bacon.

'He's not a parrot, and don't open his cage when the back door's open,' Em warned, but Hubert was not in the habit of listening to instructions. He opened the cage door and put in his fat finger with Mrs Zlotkin's handkerchief tied round it. Gabby, who had learned to trust human fingers, hopped on to it.

'Look, Mum-may, see the pretty polly!' Getting down from the chair as clumsily as he did everything else, Hubert stumbled and fell. The love-bird flew away. Hubert grabbed for him, missed, grabbed again. He tore out half the tail feathers and the bird flew drunkenly out of the back door. Gabby was never a good flier, even with a whole tail. He floundered into a tree, and the white cat got him.

Wails and shrieks. Liza swore.

'What have I done *now*?' Hubert wanted to know. 'It was the mean old cat.'

'Of course it was, my love.' Mrs Zlotkin put her fat arms round him.

Her face went blank with surprise when Em rounded on her, 'Don't blame the cat – blame that stupid Boob!'

Mrs Zlotkin had not come here to be talked to like *that*, thank you very much. After she and the Boob had flounced off in the purple van, Liza went into the wood to call Dusty from where he was hiding. He didn't come. Liza began to worry. 'He doesn't know his way round here, and he don't see so well.'

He tore out half the tail feathers

'He'll turn up at supper-time,' Michael said. 'Let's have a bird funeral to take your mind off it.'

'Only if no one is going to say anything against Maud,' Em said.

She went upstairs to get their father's long black oilskin, which she wore for funerals of mice, and frozen hedgehogs, and the kitten that had drowned in the duck pond, learning to fish for newts. They put the love-bird into a biscuit packet and buried it under the tree 'where he died so bravely'. Em read some verses from a poem they had found in a musty exercise book in what might once have been a children's nursery, long, long ago. The writing was brown and faint. Between the pages was a dried flower, and a small bird's feather.

> *Found in the garden, dead in his beauty –*
> *O, that a linnet should die in the spring!*
> *Bury him, comrades, in pitiful duty.*
> *Muffle the dinner-bell. Solemnly ring.*
>
> *Bury him nobly, next to the donkey.*
> *Fetch the old banner, and wave it about.*
> *Bury him deeply. Think of the monkey.*
> *Shallow his grave, and the dogs got him out.*
>
> *Bury him softly, white wool around him . . .*

Carrie's thoughts drifted away to the child who had written that poem more than a hundred years ago. A house full of animals then, just like now. A house made for animals. Wood's End, World's End . . .

Sleepy after the big lunch, she stood with her back to the road, her face lifted in pleasure to the sun. In the commotion of Gabby's death, Lucy had put her bearded face into the hammock and torn off the cover of *Horses in my Life* to get at the glue in the backing. Carrie would have to pay the library for it. How? . . . Somehow . . . Not bother now . . .

> *Farewell sweet singer, dead in thy beauty . . .*

Carrie began to have that feeling at the back of her neck. Creepy. The creepy feeling that someone is watching you from behind. She spun round, and nearly died of shock.

In the lane, half hidden behind the tree at the corner of the hedge, was a horrible-looking man, with a tired, panting dog on a frayed rope. Black Bernie, and the dog was Dusty!

Liza saw him at the same time. She ran across the lawn and took the rope off the dog's collar.

'Very nice, my dears. Very nice to see you young 'uns playin' your innocent games.' Leering with one eye shut from his habit of sighting down a gun barrel and the other open and bloodshot, his blackened teeth grinning in his tobacco-stained mouth, Black Bernie was even more horrible than when he was enraged.

But he had brought Dusty back. 'Found him t'other side of the wood,' he said, 'looking all round, and reckoned he was lost.' His clothes were stiff with dirt and grease. He gave off a powerful smell. 'Thought he come from here, seeing how you lot have all these here animals.' His voice was creaking and croaky, unused to being used for anything but growling and swearing and bellowing.

'Thank you,' Liza, on her knees by the dog, smiled up at him, shaking back her red hair. 'It was very kind.'

'Think nothing of it.' Was he going to ask for a reward? Was that why he had come? 'But you want to watch him. Lots of dog-stealing these days. Something dreadful. Lost a dog meself only last week.'

'A collie?' Carrie asked before she could stop herself.

But Bernie shook his head. 'Never did know one breed from t'other. Only an ignorant man, Missie. No schooling . . . Never had no chance . . .'

Whining, he put his huge knotted hand up to his unkempt hair and tugged at a piece of it – Black Bernie tugging his forelock like a peasant of olden times! – and went away, walking in the ditch at the side of the lane, shuffling among last year's leaves.

They looked at each other. 'He wasn't so bad.' Carrie frowned, not understanding.

'We were wrong to think he'd been dog-stealing,' Liza said.

The tree above them rustled and shook. Lester suddenly dropped down out of it.

Liza jumped, and said, 'I wish you wouldn't do that.'

Carrie had got used to Lester appearing and disappearing. 'He wasn't so bad, was he?' she asked him.

'He's cunning.' Lester darted out to the road to see Bernie's humped back shuffling round the corner. 'More dangerous than we thought.'

'But he brought back Dusty. If he wanted to steal dogs—'

'To put us off the scent,' Lester said. 'Hadn't you thought of that? *I think he knows we know something.*'

'We don't know much.'

'But he doesn't know *how* much. If he finds he can't choke us off like this, he'll try something else.'

Carrie stared at him.

'He could get dangerous.' Lester stared back at her, knowing she understood. 'He'll stop at nothing.'

Twenty-one

The summer holidays arrived, which was marvellous.

Hubert Zlotkin came, which was not so marvellous.

He was spoiled and greedy and useless. Bad enough when he was lying in the hammock, eating potato crisps and reading comics. Worse when he was out of it – a threat to society – because you never knew where he was going to make trouble.

'We only put up with you so that Liza can stay!' Carrie was driven to yell at him in fury, after he had left a gate open and Oliver had ambled down the road and eaten three rows of peas and some budding zinnias in the garden of the village policeman.

'That's right.' One of the worst things about Hube the Boob was that he had no pride. 'But if my Mum-may wasn't in Clacton with Minnie Boggs, I wouldn't put up with *you*. There's nothing to do in this rotten hole.'

'Try working.'

'I didn't mean *that*.' Hubert was shocked. 'I mean, I've never lived in a house without the telly. Why ain't you got a set?'

'Don't you know television needs electricity? Don't you know *anything*?'

He moaned for his favourite programmes.

'Five o'clock.' Guzzling bread and jam, he gazed mournfully at the watch nailed to the kitchen wall, which was the only clock in the house. 'Just time for *Land of the Green Monsters*.'

Hube the Boob. Hube the Boob Tube, they called him when he kept carrying on about television. Square as a Cube.

Although he was more round than square. To shut him up and get some fat off him, Tom set him to digging up a bed to plant with winter cabbages. Hubert toiled away panting, sweat pouring off him, sticking the fork through his foot, falling over backwards if he struck a root. Once he pretended to faint, very dramatically, clutching his brow and crying, 'It's all going black!' before he swooned carefully into a soft path of long grass. Tom dashed a bucket of water over his head, so he didn't try that again.

Poor old Hube. Tom got quite fond of him, because he was so awful.

'You must work if you want to eat,' he told him.

Hubert understood that. He wanted to eat.

A man from the village drove to a factory in Nettlefield every morning, so he took Tom with him to his new job at the zoo. Liza rode Old Red to the bus stop, and went to the housing estates to work for Mr Harvey.

She was clumsy and reckless and slapdash. 'But she'll learn,' Mr Harvey sighed. He called her Old Red, like the bicycle. She wore her russet hair in a thick braided rope down her back, and sometimes when she came home she was so tired that she cried when she told them what she had broken or spilled, and how many wrong medicines Mr Harvey had just stopped her giving in the nick of time, and how many wrong messages she had given to customers.

'I told this lady her dog was ready to go home,' she said. 'But it was Heaven he was ready to go home to, not her.'

'What did Mr Harvey say?'

Liza sighed and wiped her eyes with the end of her pigtail. ' "You'll learn." '

Everyone was tired, working in the heat of this amazing August. Em was baby-sitting for various local mothers who couldn't stand having their children home from school. Carrie was doing deliveries with John and the trap for a market gardener whose engine had dropped out of the bottom of his truck.

After the collapse of his muck cart, Michael had dragged home an old wicker armchair from the dump, and had converted it into a sort of horse-powered wheelchair in which he and Oliver Twist took an old crippled lady for rides. Her name was Miss Cordelia Chattaway. She paid Michael five pence a time to ride through the lush green lanes under a mauve silk parasol, bowing and smiling to non-existent friends and admirers, her wheezy old chow dog squatting on her useless little feet.

In the evenings, everyone ran up the meadow slope, through the fence and down through Mr Mismo's cow pasture to plunge into the cool shallow brook. They lay on the pebbly bottom with their eyes closed, letting the water run over them.

'It's too cold!' Hubert wailed, dipping in a toe like an uncooked cocktail sausage.

Charlie barked behind him. He started, slipped, fell in, and lay on his back like a dead fish, his pale hair floating downstream.

'I feel like the mermaid in *Mysteries of the Deep*,' he said. 'Sunday evenings, seven-thirty.'

Hube the Boob Tube. He was a step down on the ladder of human development.

'We had a monkey that was more intelligent than you,' Carrie told him.

'So what?' He lay in the cool water with his face screwed up, as if someone were going to come at him with a bar of scrubbing soap. 'Monkeys used to be people.'

He got everything wrong.

Joey the black woolly monkey was not coming home. When he recovered from pneumonia, Janet Lynch had suggested that he should stay at the Children's Zoo.

'Get sick again, if not,' she said in her clipped, time-saving way. 'If you love him, let him stay.'

Carrie missed him sadly, and would not admit that life was easier without the mess of him, and the clamouring for attention, and the scares – where was he? What had he got into?

'Not good, you know, to keep a monk at home,' Jan Lynch said. 'Needs his own kind.'

'He needed *me*,' Carrie said sadly, remembering the clutching arms, the leathery little hands, the mumbly kisses. How he chirped when he was happy. How he cried like a baby when he was unhappy, and it looked like laughing, if you didn't know.

One evening when the sun had gone down and drawn the worst of the flies with it, Carrie and Lester and Michael and the dogs went for a long supper ride with sandwiches in their pockets and a hot water bottle of cider lashed to the front of John's saddle.

They rode through the woods, where the path was black and squashy from centuries of fallen leaves, down into a valley, across a tiny stream where Oliver jumped three feet in the air from a standstill and Michael fell off, and up to the top of the gorse common to eat their sandwiches on the sinister lip of the Bottle Dump quarry.

111

In the summer, the bushes were too thick to see down to the shacks. They sent Michael sliding down the steep bank to scout. He came back to report nothing. No lights in the shacks. No dogs in sight. He had thrown down a stone to see what barked or moved.

'What did?'

'Only some rats on a rubbish heap. They went back into it. I saw their tails.'

They rode home another way, across the abandoned airfield at the top of a flat-crested hill. It was rather a spooky place, even in the daytime. In the War, in the Battle of Britain, young men had flown from here to keep the enemy away from England's shores. Young men who hadn't been pilots before the war, straight from school many of them, quickly trained, so many needed, because so many who took off from here in their tiny Spitfire fighter-planes did not come back.

The broken-down huts in the middle of the field held secret memories of those perilous times long before Carrie was born. Once when she was riding here alone, she had passed the small hut with the notice, 'Briefing Room', still on the door, where the young pilots had sat in their flight overalls and parachute harness to get last-minute orders. She thought she saw the white face of a young boy glance out of the window at her, and then look back, as if he was listening to someone inside. A piece of paper blew. John had shied. What at? When she recovered her balance, the glimpse of a face was not there. Never had been?

At twilight, the airfield was especially eerie. The breeze creaked among the loose boards of the huts, and lifted a piece of tin on a roof with the mournful sound of a cracked bell. Carrie would not have come here at dusk without Lester and the dogs. Charlie and Perpetua and Moses cast wide over the field, noses down, like hounds seeking the scent. Suddenly they all got the same scent at once and streaked across the broad field together, barking with what they thought was the cry of a pack.

What on earth? From one of the huts in the middle of the

airfield came an answering chorus of frenzied barks and howls.

'Come on!' They cantered across the field, over the broken runways, Oliver in a scuttling gallop to keep up, Michael leaning forward like a jockey. The door at the end of the hut was fastened with an iron bar and a rusty padlock. The windows were roughly boarded up. But between the boards, they could see noses of dogs, several of them, yelping and scrabbling, while Charlie and Perpetua and Moses jumped against the wall from outside, boasting their freedom.

Twenty-two

Carrie and Michael were all for breaking into the shed and setting the dogs free, but Lester said no.

'We'd be destroying the evidence against Bernie. There's nothing for it now.' He turned Peter away, neck-reining with the halter rope. 'We must bring in the Law.'

When they came round the hill into their lane, past the big stone where Peter always shied, and John shied in sympathy, even if he didn't see it, they sent Michael back to the stables and turned John and Peter (with difficulty) away from home. The village police station was a narrow brick cottage like a shoebox on end, with a flourishing garden, in spite of Oliver's raid on the peas and zinnias. Had the policeman's wife told him about that? She had said she wouldn't.

'I'll tell him it was rabbits,' she had said, and hoed out the small hoof marks and gave Carrie a cup-cake. She was well known for always being on the side of the criminal and against her husband. She had once employed a boy to chop wood, knowing he was wanted for car theft by the police of three counties.

Through the front window, uncurtained on this summer night, Lester and Carrie saw the lighted square of the television with two fat men mouthing *Smile Awhile*. One of Hubert's favourites. He repeated its rotten jokes all wrong, missing the point.

Lester got off and knocked. The policeman came to the door with his collar off, wearing enormous plaid slippers like pieces of luggage.

'Excuse me, Constable.' All the local children were very polite to Constable Dunstable, so that he would imagine they were on his side. 'Have you heard about any dogs disappearing lately?'

'What's up?' The constable turned his grizzled head halfway, so that he could look sideways at Lester suspiciously. All boys to him were bad news.

'If there has been any larceny of privately owned canines,' Lester said, very formal, 'we think we can assist you in your inquiries.'

'Who says I'm making inquiries?' He still was suspicious. 'What do you know?'

'I know where some stolen dogs are. If you'll come with us, we'll show you the evidence.'

'Don't bother me, boy.' Constable Dunstable blew out his purple-veined cheeks testily. 'I'm off duty.'

'Tomorrow morning then?'

'I'm appearing in court on a motor-cycle case.' He made it sound as if he was judge, jury and lawyers, all in one.

'That young man wasn't drunk and you know it!' his wife called from inside the house.

'We'll take you in the afternoon.'

'I'll go by myself. Where is it?'

'The road's overgrown. No one's been that way for years. We'll show you our short cut.'

Next afternoon, they rode the horses and Constable Dunstable rode his motor-bike as far as he could. When the path was too soft, he got off and wheeled it.

'Leave it here till you come back,' Carrie suggested.

'Government property, Miss Fielding.' Usually, he called her Cathy or Girl, but he was on official business now. He

114

wheeled on, squelching in loamy mud up to the hubs and ankles.

They tethered the horses at the edge of the airfield. The constable tethered his motor-bike with a chain and padlock. Lester wanted to approach the hut crawling on their stomachs through the long grass, but the policeman refused, and they marched together across the wide field to the group of derelict huts.

'Are you sure this was the one?' Carrie was puzzled. The bar was across the door of the hut, but there was no barking, no scrabbling or whining from inside.

'Look at our hoofprints. This is where the dogs were,' Lester told the policeman, who banged on the door with the flat of his hand.

Nothing.

'Open up in the name of the Law!' he shouted. His voice carried away over the empty airfield.

The dogs had gone. Vanished like the face of the young pilot Carrie had thought she had seen. But the dogs had been real. There was the hoof-trampled ground where they had discussed what to do. There were scratches on the faded paint where the dogs outside had scrabbled and yapped at the dogs inside.

'They're gone,' she said flatly.

'Very funny,' said Constable Dunstable bitterly. 'Ve-ry comical. Leading a person up the garden path, or as we say in my profession, Misrepresentation of Facts. Not a chargeable offence, but a minor misdemeanour, which I can *not* forgive. Or forget,' he added darkly, and turned away to tramp back through the uncut ungrazed grass to his bicycle. John and Peter lifted their heads to watch him make twelve angry tries to turn the key in the padlock. John curled back his top lip, showing his teeth and gums. He had eaten a bitter root, but it looked as if he was sneering at Constable Dunstable.

Michael went off that evening to take Miss Cordelia Chattaway and her chow dog for their chariot ride. He came back too soon, riding Oliver at a trot so fast you could hardly see the pony's legs, the wicker chair bouncing over the ruts and potholes.

'It's happened!' He jumped off and ran, shouting for Carrie. 'Miss Chattaway's dog – it's gone!'

'Dead?' The dog was at least twelve, and bronchial to boot.

'Stolen. She let him out last night and that's the last she saw. She has abandoned hope and gone into deep mourning. The lady next door baked her a chocolate cake.'

'Has she told the policeman?'

'I did, on the way home. He said, "If I get any more lip from you kids, I'll arrest you for vagrancy." '

They were having supper when Lester came. He tapped so gently on the window of the saloon bar that no one but Carrie heard anything more than a twig.

It was bread pudding. Liza had got the measurements wrong and baked six times as many loaves as they needed. She had taken them from door to door in a basket, but the baker had caught her and threatened to report her for trading without a licence, because her bread was better than his. So now everything had to be made with bread, and even Rosie, Redruth and Rubella, who were bullied away from the grain by the other hens, were refusing it.

Carrie picked up her pudding plate and headed for the kitchen.

'Finish it!' Liza was sometimes jokey with them, sometimes suddenly rough. You didn't always know if she meant it.

'I have.'

By the door, she slid the lump of pudding inside her shirt and turned round to show the empty plate. Outside, waiting for Lester to show where he was, she held out the waist of her shorts and sucked in her stomach to let the lump of pudding fall to the ground. Charlie sniffed at it suspiciously and backed off.

'They'd need best steak to steal *him* away,' Lester said.

'But you know who they *have* stolen?' Carrie went in under the weeping willow, where Lester was squatting under the tent of feathery falling branches. As she told him about Miss Cordelia Chattaway's chow dog, she could see his mind beginning to work just as clearly as if lights were flashing in his head and bells ringing.

It was a thrilling and hazardous plan.

'If there's only room for one, who will it be?' Carrie whispered, although she could hear the others on the other side of the house, sailing the duck pond on a raft made out of a door.

'Me.'

'Who says?'

'You muffed it once.'

'When?' Carrie glared.

'Asking that question about the collie. He knows we know. That's why he moved the dogs from Bottle Dump.'

'And from the airfield. I suppose some of those hoof marks weren't made by *your* horse?'

'I'm the eldest.'

'You're not.' She could never find out exactly how old he was. When she asked his mother, Mrs Figg had said, 'As old as his tongue and a little older than his teeth,' which was so perfectly infuriating that Carrie had not asked again. 'We'll toss.'

Lester had everything in his pockets but money, so he took two smooth yellow willow twigs of different lengths and held them in a fist, staring at Carrie to try and make her choose the wrong one.

She picked the longest twig. 'I won.'

'Shortest wins.'

'It's always the longest! That's cheating.'

He laughed. 'Just seeing if I could get away with it.' One of the things about Lester was that if he lost a toss or a contest, he didn't argue or lose interest. The plan was just as exciting as when he thought he was going to be the one who hid in the boot of the Poacher's car.

He had the little hairbrush in his pocket. He and Carrie

117

banged it on the backs of their hands, whirled them about to make the blood start, and then pressed them together, mingling vows in blood to seal the secret.

'I swear.'

Twenty-three

Miss Cordelia Chattaway's chow dog was called Lancelot.

'That *was* his name,' she told Carrie sorrowfully. 'Not *is*. I am certain that he has met his death, and can only hope that it was swift and painless.' She sat in her garden in a high-backed basket chair like a sentry box, with a rug over her crippled legs. 'Good afternoon, Vicar!' She nodded to a crow which had landed on the bird-bath. 'I'm afraid you find me in sad heart.' She was a little dotty.

'You don't think he's been stolen?' Carrie sprawled by her tiny feet which did not reach the ground, and chewed grass.

'Why would anyone want to steal Lancelot?'

Carrie did not tell her. The thought of the poor amiable old chow injected with some disease, operated on, put to some strain to see how much his groggy heart could stand . . .

'Don't give up hope, Miss Chattaway.'

'I have.' Under a big floppy hat with grey ribbons, the little face was set in grief. For three days now Carrie had waited in the bushes at Bottle Dump for a sight of the Poacher's car. She was going back there this evening, and tomorrow, and tomorrow, until she could find Lancelot and bring back Miss Chattaway's smile.

There had been a postcard several days ago:

'Great Cruise.

Will come and see you before we set out for the Roaring Forties.'

On the front, there was a photograph of a small ketch with a line of laundry in the rigging and a potted geranium on the main hatch, in a harbour full of bigger, grander boats. A woman in a brief swimsuit leaned against the mast with her fair hair blowing.

'Looks a bit like your mum.' Bessie Munce took her spectacles out of the stamp drawer and peered.

'It is.'

'In that bathing suit? Oh my.' The postmistress handed the card over quickly, as if it were infected.

'Soon' could mean any old time. They had made up the bed in their mother's room and spent two days' food money on buying a big ham. Liza cooked it and hung it in a pillowcase from the hook in the rafter where Gabby's cage had

119

hung. Partly because for centuries that had always been the place for hams in this house. Partly to keep it safe from the cats.

Late in the evening, when Carrie was back from a useless vigil at the quarry, their parents arrived after dark in a car with one headlight, a smoking radiator and no top.

'What do you do when it rains?' Michael asked.

'Put on foul weather gear, and your mother bales out with the ashtray.'

He was brown and fit and grinning through his dark curly beard as he tried to hug everybody at once. Mother looked as if life at sea agreed with her after all. She wasn't thin and pale any more. She stood up straight and there was wind and sun tan on her cheeks, instead of smudges of tiredness. Her hair was longer and lighter.

'Did you bleach it for the photographs?' Em asked.

'The sun did. We sent that swimsuit picture to the *Daily Amazer*, and the editor sent back a view of St Paul's, and wrote on the back: "Whee-wheew!"'

While they were laughing and hugging and all talking at once, Liza waited in the background, looking don't care-ish, so as not to look shy.

'Who's the gorgeous bird?' Dad asked.

'Liza Jones. We wrote and told you.'

'You said a new friend. I thought it was a cow, or an armadillo.'

'Liza.' Mother unwound her legs from Michael's arms, and went to her and kissed her.

Liza was stiff at first, because she didn't trust mothers, but when Dad hugged her, she relaxed. You had to, when he hugged, or get your ribs broken. They went into the house, and Michael stood on his father's shoulders to get down the ham. The endless stale bread had finally been thrown to the ducks, so there was a fresh cottage loaf, like a fat brown lady with a tiny head, and the tomato plants on the sunny wall had yielded up some small yellowish fruit. They all sat round the big table in the kitchen, with cats and dogs in a greedy outer ring.

Mother had brought a lot of food, some of which Dad recognized as stolen from the stores of *The Lady Alice*, which was sailing out for the Seven Seas next week.

'We'll starve to death before we hit the Horse Latitudes,' he grumbled.

The word 'horse' triggered Carrie off. 'Ships that took horses to the West Indies got becalmed there,' she said, 'and the horses died of thirst. Once there was a mare who was going to have a foal, and there was exactly six inches of rainwater in her bucket. Well, days went by, and the sailors were throwing the dead horses overboard . . .'

As Carrie started into a long-winded horse story, her father automatically put his hand over the ear with the gold ring in it, just as if he had never been away. Looking past her, his eyes became fixed in a stare of disbelief. What had he seen?

In the doorway, stout in one of the tent-shaped nightgowns Mrs Zlotkin had sent with him, hair standing up in spikes, fat pink mouth pulled down in sleepy sulks . . .

'You woke me up!' Hubert whined.

'One, two, three, four.' Jerome Fielding counted his children. 'If we had a third son, Alice, would that be him?'

'Come and have some cake, Hubie, old Boob.' Tom got up and brought the blubbery figure to the table. 'It's Liza's brother. See the likeness?'

Liza howled and threw an orange at him. Hubert wailed, 'If I looked like *her* I'd shoot myself!' The dogs barked, and Nobody, the striped cat on Em's lap, put out a swift paw and hooked down a piece of ham.

Next day they all went to the zoo in the chancy car, which Dad had borrowed from 'a man I rescued from drowning'. The starter switch was broken, so he had to lift the bonnet and connect the red starter wire to the black ground wire. The car leaped into life, Hubert lost his balance and knocked it into gear, and Dad had to run with it and hop in over the stuck door, as it moved off without him.

Hubert complained of the heat, the cold, the wind, the

noise, the engine smell, and when Dad cornered on two wheels, he nearly fell out, and had to be clutched by the broad seat of his shorts.

'I'm dizzy!' he wailed. Being dizzy was one of his favourite illnesses. His mother took him to the special doctor, and then for a chocolate fudge sundae to make up for the doctor finding nothing wrong. 'I'm dizzy!'

'Put a sock in it, brat,' Dad said, and Em, who always echoed him, said, 'Stop breathing, Boob.'

Tom was in the Children's Zoo. He was with the baby elephant, which had to have someone with it all the time, to make up for losing its mother. Tom stood with an arm fondly over its back, the way Michael stood with his pony. It had a trunk like the hose of a vacuum cleaner, and bristly hair that made Hubert jump back six feet. 'It pricked my fingers!'

'Oh, put a sock in it.'

Hubert was afraid of the chimpanzees, and disgusted by the snakes, and gave sweets to all the animals that had a sign up: 'DO NOT FEED.'

'Pooh, what a pong,' he said to the lion, and a big angora goat came up behind him and butted the wide target of his back view. Hube the Boob. You thought he couldn't get any more awful, and then he did.

Although she hated zoos, Carrie liked to spend time here with the animals; but today she was restless, thinking all the time of the adventure ahead. Tomorrow? Day after? Next week? She would have to go every day to Bottle Dump until the Poacher came.

Her mother asked her, 'What's on your mind?' They were in the monkey house. Carrie was cuddling Joey, who had held out his arms and chirped gladly when he saw her.

'What do you mean?' Always answer a tricky question with another question.

'I know you. You're up to something.'

'Well, we're always *up* to something,' Carrie said. 'Life would be pretty dull if not.'

'Something good?'

'Mm-hm.' Carrie nodded, digging her chin into the top of the monkey's woolly head. The saving of life. All those dogs, the old chow, shut up somewhere, perhaps already in the laboratories, still waiting for their own people. Don't let it be too late . . .

'Tell me?' Her mother turned away and bent towards a cage, making faces at the owl monkey, who stared back with round amber eyes. She knew when to be casual. And she knew about what people had to do for animals. She had understood about rescuing John, and about Joey. She had once been arrested in Spain for unharnessing and leading away a lame cab horse while the driver was in a bar, and Dad had practically torn down the police station until they let her out of the cell.

She knew about danger. Hadn't she risked her life to save Michael in the fire?

There are these dogs, you see. I've got to save them . . . Carrie could only tell it in her head, because she had sworn in blood to keep the secret.

Twenty-four

And then that evening, it all happened.

As soon as their parents left, Carrie rode over the common to the Headless Horseman's precipice, and down the hill into the clump of trees where she tied John. If she was not home by a certain time, Lester would ride here and lead him back, knowing she had gone on her perilous mission.

She crept forward through the bushes, adding more bramble scratches to the ones already criss-crossing her brown arms and legs. When she got to the pile of stones where she could hide and watch the shacks, she lay down.

Something warm lay down beside her. Something wet licked her arm.

'*Charlie!*' He rolled up his eyes and grinned. He had been told to stay at home. She had last seen him drooping by the gate, head down, tail down, watching mournfully through the bars, as if he was not planning to wriggle through as soon as she was round the corner, and trail her.

'Lie still.' She put a hand on his curly shoulder, and raised herself up to look through a chink in the stones. At last. There it was. The bulky, battered car with the crooked bumpers and the rust stains that looked like blood, and the boot yawning half open, tied down with a piece of wire.

This is it.

She took Charlie back to John, made him lie down and told him sternly, 'Stay. You *stay*.' Charlie put his head on his paws and licked his lips. 'Lester will come for you,' she told them.

She crept back to a sheltered place near the Poacher's car, took a deep breath, then dashed out, bent double, unhooked the wire, crawled into the boot and hooked up the wire again.

She crouched at the back of the filthy, cluttered space, her heart pounding, sick with excitement.

The two men came out of the shack together.

'Come up, you brute,' Bernie growled, and there was a choking noise, as if he was dragging a dog by the neck.

'This chow-chow's hardly worth it,' the Poacher grumbled in his whining voice. 'Thing's half dead.'

'It's a dog, ain't it? Got a liver and kidneys and four legs. They shoot the legs off 'em, you know,' Black Bernie said chattily, 'to give the Army docs practice at war wounds.'

The Poacher laughed, a high braying sound that was worse than Bernie's hoarse chuckle.

'If there's any sign of anyone snooping round your place – *get* in that car, you fat beast – you'll have to move the dogs. Them lousy kids ... man can't make an honest living.'

The Poacher made a sound like 'Gurrutcher' and got into

the car. The door slammed and the engine started, shaking the whole car and knocking Carrie about among the tools, crumpled newspapers, beer bottles, oily rags and something that might once have been part of a bird. As the car backed over the rough ground, she bumped her head on the same place where she had hit it and got a concussion when she fell off Peter.

With a lurch that knocked her elbow on a piece of metal and set the nerves screaming, the Poacher started forward. She lay cramped and breathless, watching the road through the gap below the bouncing top of the boot. She must know exactly where they went.

Charlie jumped out of the trees, hurtled down a bank and galloped after her down the road.

'Go back!' she shouted, but the engine noise was enough to drown her voice from the dog as well as the Poacher. He would not obey anyway, if he had set his mind on this. *Go back!* She tried to will him to turn, as she could often think him into turning round when he was trotting ahead of her.

The thought waves didn't work. The only hope was that he would get tired and give up. The Poacher turned into a straighter road and put on speed, the exhaust roaring like a dragon. The dog became smaller, desperately running, then a speck, then there was nothing on the black road. *Go home, Charlie.*

The drive seemed endless. Bruised and battered, her head aching, Carrie tried to remember how they went – turn right, turn left, past a school, over a hump-backed bridge (My poor head!) past that lopsided haystack . . .

The Poacher braked suddenly, shooting Carrie forward among the tools. He turned through a gate and jolted up a long rutted path between fields, with Carrie thrown back among the bits of bird. Down a sharp dip, and he stopped at last. The engine panted for a moment and died. There was a sound of muffled barking. The dog in the car answered wheezily. The Poacher cursed at it and yanked it out of the car.

Carrie waited. There were no footsteps on the soft

125

ground. When she heard him at the door of the place where the dogs were, she would slip out and hide somewhere till he . . .

A hand with horn-thick nails came in through the opening of the boot, unhooked the wire and flung open the top.

Carrie thought afterwards that they both screamed together. She thought – but she could not afterwards remember anything clearly – that as she somehow scrambled out, he grabbed a piece of iron and hit her on the head (poor old head, same place again). She fell. The man stood over her in his baggy clothes, his eyes crazed, his mouth twisted. She saw the spanner in his raised hand, heard dogs barking, one bark familiar and frantic, as a panting mass of fur leaped out of nowhere at the Poacher's back.

Caught from behind, the small man went down. Charlie had him by the coat, worrying it like a rat. The man wriggled free of the loose jacket, Charlie yelped as a boot went into his ribs, and then the coat was over his head, the sleeves tied, and he was thrown into the car. The Poacher jumped in and drove off furiously, scattering mud as he shot up the slope and roared away down the other side.

Carrie struggled up and started to limp after him, shouting. Her legs gave way and she dragged herself to the top of the slope on hands and knees. Far away, the car turned off the field track on to the road, shot ahead with a squeal of worn tyres, and was gone.

Dizzy and sick, Carrie sat down and held her head. She had no idea where she was. She could not remember the way they had come. She did not know this view. A vast cornfield, dark gold in the low sunlight, ripe for the reaper.

As she gazed, the cornfield shimmered, misted, wavered into nothing, as she toppled over and blacked out.

When she opened her eyes, the sun was down and every inch of her skin was being eaten by midges. She sat up and looked back into the dip. The Poacher's jerry-built caravan stood lopsided under the trees. The dogs inside it were still barking hoarsely. Miss Cordelia Chattaway's chow dog was

126

*She saw the spanner in his raised hand, heard one bark,
familiar and frantic . . .*

sitting on the orange crate which was the doorstep, waiting to see what would happen next.

Weaving dizzily, scratching her scratched arms, Carrie went down to the caravan. The chow stood up, wagging his curled tail expectantly, as if it was his own back door. Inside, the dogs barked. There was a padlock. She took a big stone and began to beat on it, missing sometimes, and once dropping the stone on her bare foot. When she smashed the padlock and undid the latch, two large dogs jumped out past her, knocking the chow from the orange crate, and took off up the slope. The fat old chow waited, panting and drooling, to see what would happen next.

'Come on, Lancelot.' Carrie turned her back on the wretched caravan, which stank of the Poacher and his trade and the dogs shut up in there.

They went slowly up the slope and down the long field track, the chow wheezing, Carrie half dragging him along, half supporting herself on him. Her head was throbbing. Her arms and legs felt like cooked spaghetti. Once or twice she fell, grazing hands and knees, and the dog waited, panting, until she got up and stumbled on to the road.

Which way? The Poacher's car had turned left. Or was it right? It seemed too long ago to remember. The skid marks in the gravel were on the left. She turned and began walking somewhere . . . anywhere.

She did not know how long she had walked when a passing car stopped. A man leaned out. 'Why must you walk in the middle of the road?' he asked.

'Was I?'

'You look rough,' he said. 'I suppose I ought to give you a lift.'

Never take lifts from strange men. Dimly at the back of her head sounded the well-worn message that must have been for somebody else. She got into the car with Lancelot.

'Where are we?' she asked. It was getting dark.

'Search me.' The man wore a neat suit and a prim felt hat.

'I'm a stranger here myself, headed through for the north. Where do you want to go?'

'Home.'

He sighed. 'Where's that?'

Carrie was blank. She beat her fist on the good side of her head, and came up with the name of the village.

'Never heard of it. Which way is it?'

'I don't know where I am.'

The man looked at her. 'What's the matter with you?'

'I was in a fight.'

He put up a hand. 'Don't tell me about it. There's too much trouble these days.'

'The man got Charlie.' The pain of that was unbearable.

'He probably asked for it,' the man said stupidly, 'whoever he was. Count me out. I don't want to get mixed up.'

He was quite nervous. When they came to a small town, he stopped at a lighted doorway where some people were coming out of a cinema.

'Better get out,' he said, 'and ask the way.'

'Will you wait?' Carrie opened the door and got out with the dog.

'I'd like to get on. I'm not going your way.'

Before she could ask him how he could know that, until he knew which *was* her way, he drove off, his hat square and prim on his nervous head.

There were some young men and girls fooling about in front of the cinema. They stopped and stared at Carrie and Lancelot. 'The Lady and the Tramp,' one of them said, and they all laughed.

Carrie asked them if they knew the way to her village.

'We're going that way.' The boy had a lot of long, pale hair, like the mane of a lion. 'We'll take you if you can stand a crush.'

The crush was squeezing in beside the boy's bony girl-friend in the side-car of a motor-bike, with the chow like a mammoth suet pudding on their feet. Carrie fell asleep, and woke with the girl's sharp elbow in her ribs.

'Where do you live?' They were in the village. They took her out to World's End and rode off, their hair like streamers in the night wind.

As Carrie went into the stable yard, Lester jumped from the loft door of the barn down into the pile of straw.

'You got him. You marvel, I knew you would. When you didn't come back, I went for John. What about the other dogs?'

'I let them loose.'

'Oh, you *marvel*.'

'They got Charlie.' Carrie almost never cried. She did now. Lester hugged her, but she could not stop crying.

Twenty-five

One of the dogs that Carrie had let loose turned up at his home two days later. The other was picked up by the police, raiding dustbins, and the Cruelty Man was keeping him in the kennels until he could find the owner.

Miss Cordelia Chattaway changed her black gown for her rambler rose Sunday dress, and wanted Michael to take her and Lancelot for a ride again, but Michael wouldn't. No one could do anything, with Charlie in danger.

Carrie could not tell anybody about being hit. They would send for Mother, and she might send for the doctor who had murmured over Carrie's concussion, and he would murmur her into bed, with chicken broth and the curtains drawn.

She thought of Charlie all the time, woolly and grinning, with his badly-fitting brown eyes that showed the white all round, and rolled when he was gay. Her head ached most of the time. Lester brought some aspirin from his mother's medicine cabinet at Mount Pleasant.

'What for?' Carrie blinked and frowned under the weight of her headache.

'Why didn't you tell me the Poacher hit you?'

'He didn't—' she began, but Lester put out his hand and gently touched the lump under her hair, that no one else had seen.

'Poached egg,' he said.

The Poacher had disappeared. His caravan had gone, leaving a litter of bones and beer bottles, and he was not seen again in those parts. Black Bernie had also vanished. His friend (if he had ever had a friend) One-Eyed Jake the Pig Man, gave the information that he had gone away for his health and would not be back until goodness knows when – if then, since the damp at the Dump was getting to his joints.

The Cruelty Man had been to all the dealers he knew. None of them had seen Charlie. None would admit to knowing either Bernie or the Poacher.

'Why would they take him to a dealer?'

'Well ... You know why, Carrie. We've been into this before. The University only buys through regular dealers.' He did not want to talk about the Research Laboratories.

'If they didn't sell him for the Labradors,' Michael said, 'what else would they do?'

The Cruelty Man was sitting on the old lawn roller, which was one of the garden seats, consoling himself with a mug of cider after a fruitless trip to the other end of the county. Michael stood in front of him, his small, hard-working hand on his knee, his clear eyes searching the man's crinkly ones for an honest answer.

'What else would they do with our dog?'

'You know that too, Mike. If Charlie attacked the Poacher again—'

'Which he would.'

'—a gutless sort of bloke like that wouldn't take any risks.'

'He'd kill him, you mean.'

The Cruelty Man nodded, looking glumly into his cider

131

mug, and Carrie said, 'It would be better than the – than the other thing.'

One of the girls at Mount Pleasant had once worked in a laboratory, cleaning the mouse cages. She had told Liza about a mongrel dog she saw, running, running on a treadmill, with wires in its heart to check how much strain it could stand.

Hubert enjoyed tragedy, as a change from the monotony of life, which he made monotonous by being Hubert. 'Do you remember,' he sighed from the ground where he was lying on his stomach with the only two cushions, 'do you remember how Charlie could catch biscuits backwards, without looking? Alas, never again.'

'Shut up, Tube,' Em growled.

'And do you remember,' his sigh blew an insect away through the grass, 'how he'd carry that hamster about and it was always soaking? I bet it'll pinc away now that—'

'Shut *up*, I said!' Em turned him over roughly with her foot and he lay on his back like a beetle, legs waving.

'She kicked me! Li*zer*! She kicked me!'

Liza threw a book at him.

She and Tom hated having to go to work while the others searched for Charlie; calling, calling over the countryside, going again and again, uselessly, to Bottle Dump and the hollow where the Poacher's caravan had been.

It was a dreadful time. It was the most horrible time of their lives, even worse than after the fire, when their home was gone and their mother in hospital. Then at least they had known the worst. Now they knew nothing.

One night when Carrie could not sleep, she was writing in her horse book with a candle on a chair by the bed. To take her mind off Charlie, she was writing about flies – how horses could twitch any square inch of skin they wanted, while people could only do that with their faces.

'*A horse,*' she wrote, '*has to have a tail to flick and skin to twitch because he has no hands. He does not use his tail like a dog, he . . .*'

A dog . . . a dog . . . my Charlie with the shaggy hair. She

132

could feel a poem coming on, with the same sort of flushed, sick feeling that tells you a temperature is coming on, or your dinner is coming up, or both.

Her hand moved almost by itself, as if it had its own life:

I dream of Charlie with the shaggy hair,
Charlie, who saved my life by being there.
Where did they take you? Where are you now, old
*   friend?*
Can you not find the scent back to World's End?

As she read it aloud, a figure in a torn vest and drooping pyjama bottoms appeared in the doorway, trailing the mutilated voodoo doll.

'Who are you talking to?' Michael grumbled, still half asleep. 'Did Charlie come back?'

He climbed on to the bed and Carrie read the poem to him. She thought it was rather good, but small boys never say if anything is good or bad.

'You can have it for your dog book.' She tore out the page, since it did not belong with horses.

The next day, Michael went out on Oliver with a bread and dripping sandwich and a medicine bottle of water coloured with beetroot juice labelled: 'EMERJENC RASON.' He was not home by the evening.

Em came back from the wood where she had been searching, with half a dozen cats dashing up and down trees, in case Charlie had got caught in the undergrowth on his way home. Lester came back with Peter from one more useless trip to the airfield. Carrie and John came back from a long ride to a distant town, where the blacksmith had told her he had once heard there was a pet shop. He had heard wrong.

Liza came back from work with a wound on her wrist because a cat had bitten her, and a wound on her pride because Alec Harvey had said, 'That'll teach you to hold 'em the right way.' Tom came back from the zoo.

'Where's Mike?'

133

'He'll be back for supper.'

'What supper?' No one bothered to cook much these days. They lived on snacks, and Hubert spent half his time in Mrs Mismo's kitchen, trying to keep his strength up.

Carrie went to Michael's tiny room to see if he had left a note, as he sometimes did: 'Gon to vilage for comiks.' 'Gon to dig wurms for Erny MkNab farther.'

No note on the grubby flat pillow under the sloping ceiling (Michael had got this room because he was small enough to sit up in bed without crashing his head), but his marbled *Dog Lores* book was on the floor under the bed.

He had copied out Carrie's poem:

I drem of Carly with the shaggy hare
Carly who saved my life by beimg tere.
Were did the take you? Were our you know odd frend?
Can you not find the sent back to world end?

On the next page, he had written:

A dog folow his nose home unless he smel somting beter.

Had Michael got a new idea about Charlie? Carrie ran down and got on Old Red, which staggered like a groggy horse when you mounted, and squee-clunked down the lane and up the rutted track to the village rubbish tip, favourite calling place of the dogs and the goat. It was in the hollow of a dry stream, thickly set with trees and brambles and bushes which had sprung up, fertilized with garbage, to hide the garbage's ugliness. Behind a pile of brushwood and tree roots, Michael sat in the dusk like a small garden statue, his empty medicine bottle upturned on a twig. The piebald pony stood near him, eating leaves, his long white tail firmly caught in a thorn bush.

'Why didn't you come back for help?' Carrie began to work carefully to free Oliver's tail.

'You told me, if a horse gets caught up, don't let him panic. If I left him, Ollie would panic.'

134

'He wouldn't.'

'You told me.'

The strong thorns were so tangled in the pony's long tail that Carrie had to go home and get scissors. Next day, Michael trotted off again to search another rubbish tip, the back view of Oliver unfamiliar with his thick tail cut off above the hocks, swinging faster than usual, like a shortened pendulum.

A week had gone by. Then two weeks. Almost three. Soon school would start and they would have only evenings and weekends to search. Soon they would have to admit that if Charlie was trapped somewhere, caught by the neck, fallen down an old well, he would have starved by now. Soon ... eventually, they would have to give up.

'But I knew a dog once,' Mr Mismo said (he always knew something to go one better – or worse), 'that was lost for seven and one-quarter months. Woman lost it out shopping in a crowd, and she was so frenzied, she went to the Hebrides Islands, casting off the world. Her hair was already grey with sorrow, when blow me if she didn't look out of the window of her wee croftie one morning and see something in the water, and there was that dog swimming out to the island, carrying the woman's shopping basket which she'd left behind in her frenzy.'

No one could raise a smile.

'Tell you what,' he said. 'We'll take a drive to cheer you up.'

Mr Mismo's driving was bad enough even when you were happy. Usually his wife would not let him near the wheel, but she was off visiting her sister in the Isle of Wight. 'I've got to fetch some churns at the station. Come on. I'll take you all into town.'

They made excuses, but he wanted their company. You could see why, as they got to the busier roads. Crammed into the front of his dusty farm truck, because the back was full of chicken crates, Carrie, Lester, Em, Michael and Hubert (trembling like a jelly) clung to each other and tried not to scream, as Mr Mismo crawled nervously along in the

135

outside lane, with other drivers hooting and flashing their lights and taking hair's breadth chances to get past him.

He sat like a rock behind the wheel, his tweed hat tipped over his eyes and a piece of hay between his teeth to remind him of home.

'Look at that fellow!' he said, as a lorry roared past him on the wrong side, with the driver and his mate glaring and shaking their fists. 'Makes you wonder how some people passed their driving tests.'

'How did *you*?' Em asked faintly.

'Years ago when I got mine, we didn't need all these fancy tests.'

Carrie's head throbbed. Hubert moaned softly, too far gone to complain that he was hot or cold or sick or bored, as he usually did in a car.

They came through the suburbs and into the depressing outskirts of the town. Factories and warehouses, junkyards, coalyards, a grey brick prison and rows and rows of poor mean houses and narrow streets, laid like a dirty blanket over what had once been rolling countryside.

'There you are.' Mr Mismo waved his hand as if he had invented the scene. 'Bit of city life to cheer you up.'

Steering with one hand, he swerved, went up on the pavement, swerved again as a lamp-post loomed, and just scraped through between the lamp-post and the wall of the warehouse.

He stopped and mopped his face with a Union Jack handkerchief. 'That was a close one.'

His passengers opened their eyes again. 'We're on the pavement,' someone said helpfully.

'Tell you what.' Mr Mismo was steaming and bothered. 'Let's go home and not trouble with the station. They won't have my churns anyway, if I know them.' He got into gear with a crunch, and drove slowly along between the lamp-posts and the wall.

'Hadn't we better get back on the road?' someone else suggested.

'To tell the truth, old chumps,' he stopped again, 'I'm a

wee bit nervous today. Shouldn't have had those raw onions for lunch, in this heat.' His red face was dripping. The ribbon round his hat with the blue jay's feather in it was dark with sweat. 'And Mrs Mossman always drives in traffic.'

'I can drive,' Lester said.

'You've not passed a driving test.'

'Nor have you.'

'You'll get us all pinched.'

'Better than getting killed.'

'You may have a point there, son.' Mr Mismo was always reasonable.

Lester sat on a pile of sacks from the back so that he would look tall enough, and put on Mr Mismo's hat to age him and partly hide his face. Mr Mismo instructed him how to drive ('Left hand down, sound your hooter, change down *now*'), as Lester drove skilfully and safely back through the mean streets to the broader suburbs.

They passed a sign they had not seen on the way in, since they had been on the other side of the road and shielding their eyes and clutching each other and jamming their feet on the floorboards, as if they could brake by remote control. The sign pointed down a tree-lined avenue of new buildings. It pointed to the University Medical School. Lester stopped.

'You must learn to use the brakes like you use the reins,' Mr Mismo said, back in his old bossy form now that he was in the passenger seat. 'Ve-ry gentle, as if the rein was a piece of cotton thread.'

Lester looked over his shoulder at Carrie, in the back seat between Em and Michael, with Hubert stuffed down on the floor to stop him telling Lester he was dizzy.

The Cruelty Man had said that the University only bought dogs through dealers. The dealers had said they knew nothing about Charlie. But . . .

Neither she nor Lester nodded. They just looked at each other, and without a word, Lester backed a few yards and turned up the avenue.

'Wrong way,' Mr Mismo said. 'For'ard boy, for'ard.'

'Just got to deliver a message,' Lester said. 'Won't be a moment.'

They stopped behind a wall outside the car park, so that no one could see Lester driving. They left Mr Mismo in the car while they went along a path between buildings, following a sign that said 'ANIMAL RESEARCH CENTRE'. They took Hubert with them, because he was the cleanest (he used all the hot water), and also the only one who was not barefooted and wearing a torn shirt and shorts that were blue jeans cut off ragged above the knee.

'But I ain't going in there,' he said.

Through the glass doors at the entrance, they could see a woman at the reception desk who looked as if she had come from the hairdresser five minutes ago and would not be able to type with those nails.

'If you don't, I'll put spiders in your bed.'

'No, Lester, please!'

'Worms in your cocoa.'

'Carrie!'

'Earwigs in your shoes.'

'Don't, Em!'

'Maggots in your—' Michael began, and with a gulp, Hubert pushed through the doors and rolled awkwardly over the thick carpet.

The woman looked up and moved the lipstick shape of her mouth. Hubert stood in front of her, wriggling and scratching his bottom. They were talking. As soon as they saw that she was not throwing him out, the others slid through the glass doors and came in behind him silently, like a file of Indians.

'About a dog?' The woman would be frowning, if she was not afraid to crack her make-up. 'I don't understand.'

Hubert was stammering, his ears on fire, so Carrie said, 'What he means is—'

'Go away, urchins,' the woman said, 'and play somewhere else.'

'We're with him.'

138

'Indeed?' Her look was like picking up something disgusting between thumb and finger.

'We lost a dog. We thought he might be here.'

'There are a lot of dogs here,' the woman said coldly.

'Where do they come from?'

'These days, we have to get them where we can.'

'Any shaggy ones?' Michael stepped forward, shirt tail hanging out, smudge on his nose, doughnut crumbs from the last meal but one in the corners of his mouth. 'Like those sort of rugs you have beside the bed to put your feet out on to when it's cold?'

'I have a fitted carpet. Go away, little boy, or I'll have to call one of the doctors.'

'We'd like to see a doctor.' They edged towards the corridor behind the desk.

'You go one step farther and I'll call the police!' The woman put her hand on the telephone.

'We'll tell them what you do!' Suddenly Carrie heard herself shouting, exploding with anger. 'You take animals that trust people, you spray hairspray into their eyes to see if it makes them go blind, you make them run and run till they have a heart attack, you bleed them white, you—'

'Calm yourself.' The woman patted her stiff hair, or wig, or whatever it was. 'Experiments with animals save people's lives.'

'Why don't they experiment on people to save animals' lives?'

'Would you rather it was that way?' She was deeply shocked.

'Yes.'

'Now listen, you gang of hoodlums, I'm going to have to tell you a few truths.'

'Tell *him*.' They pushed Hubert into a chair by the desk. 'He's the cleverest. He can understand.'

'All right, now listen to me. Suppose you were trying to find a cure for – let's say hiccups.'

'That's easy,' Hubert said. 'You drink beer out of the wrong side of the glass.'

139

'No, no, suppose you were looking for some particular medicine—'

'I'd go to that drawer where my mum keeps the stomach powders.'

He was so stupid, it was a gift. While the woman was leaning forward, patiently trying to explain, the four others tiptoed away behind her back, dashed down the corridor, round a corner, through a door and into another corridor that smelled faintly of dog.

'Follow your nose!' Lester cried, and they burst through another door and into a concrete passage lined with barred runs. As soon as they came through the door, a great hullabaloo started up as dogs of all sizes and breeds and no breed at all hurled themselves at the gates, barking and yelping and howling and wagging their tails as if their masters had come at last.

'Shut up, pack, it's not feeding time!' A little man like a jockey with a nut-brown face and a dirty overall came out of a room at the end. 'Oy-oy!' He grabbed at the children, who were dashing from gate to gate, although if Charlie was here, they would know his voice. He caught Michael by the back of the collar. 'How did you lot get in here?'

'Past the reception desk,' Lester said, which was true.

'In the normal way.' Carrie never could help adding some detail that made it not quite true.

'What do you want?' He tried to look fierce, but his face was made for smiling, although he had no teeth to do it with, just a wide grinning gap.

'We're looking for our dog.' They could not look at the dogs in the barred runs. They could not meet their eyes.

'What breed of dog? Pedigree? Mongrel?'

'A sort of pedigree mongrel.' They told him all the good breeds that might have gone into Charlie. Michael, half choked, added the bit about the bedside rug.

'Don't tell me!' The man let him go so suddenly that he fell on his hands and scarred knees. 'Did he have a torn ear and some nasty cuts on his head?'

'He might have.'

140

'And sort of round eyes like toffee balls—'

'With a lot of white showing.'

'Oh Gawd,' said the little nut-brown man, 'that sounds like Trumpeter.'

'Our dog is Charlie.'

'Trumpeter, Joyful, Nimrod – I call 'em all that, to remind me of my days at the foxhound kennels.'

'Does he—' Carrie could hardly ask it. 'Does he sort of lift the side of his mouth, and – sort of – grin at you?'

'My Gawd,' he said, 'that's him. Went up today.'

'Went where?'

'Surgical unit. Artery transplant. Oh no you don't.' He stepped in front of them as they headed for the far end of the passage. 'No one goes through that door. Cost me my job, that would.'

'How can you *do* such a job?' Carrie raged, raising her hands as if she would hit him.

'Someone has to take care of 'em, missie, till they—'

'Look at that dog!' Lester yelled suddenly. The man stepped aside to look down the line of runs, and before he knew it, Carrie, Lester, Em and Michael were through the door and running down a corridor, up a flight of stairs, down another, across a hall lined with doors that had glass peepholes. There were cages of animals in most of the rooms. Monkeys, guinea-pigs, hamsters, rabbits, rats, mice.

A young woman in a white coat came out of one of the rooms, carrying two large cases of white mice. 'What on earth—?'

'Urgent message for the doctor,' Lester said quickly.

'Which doctor?'

'In the surgical unit.' Lester tried to sound calm, but Carrie could see that his breath was coming very fast, and his heart pounding under his thin shirt.

'You're going the wrong – hi, wait!' as they doubled back, but she could not catch up with them, because of the mice.

Back up the stairs, across a bridge to another building, through swing doors – 'I smell ether!' Lester stopped, his

141

nose twitching like – Oh, *Charlie*. Would they be too late?

'You are ze pupils from ze zgool?' They turned and saw a bent, wild-haired old gent in a flapping coat and thick spectacles, like the mad doctors in monster films. 'Come to hear ze legture about ze life zycle of the giant ztag beedle, eh? Gum, my dears.'

As he shooed them along the corridors, they passed a big door with a thick glass window. Standing on tiptoe, they saw people in white, moving expertly, stainless steel sinks, tables, cabinets full of shining instruments, gas cylinders, a huge arc light like the eye of God.

On a high table under the light, a rough-haired dog was lying calmly and trustfully. A man with a white surgical mask over his mouth and nose, holding a syringe, was stroking the dog's head and talking to him.

'Gum along, gum *along*,' the mad doctor fussed. The door said NO ENTRY. Carrie, Lester, Em and Michael entered. Charlie jerked up his head, the man dropped the syringe and the whole room fell apart, equipment and people scattering, bottles breaking, stools overturning, as the dog and the children leaped at each other, shrieking and barking with joy.

'What's going on?' The man in the mask bent to pick up his broken syringe.

'We've found our dog!'

Charlie pushed against the door with his paws and was off, and the mad doctor jumped aside just in time, as Carrie, Lester, Em and Michael raced after him to freedom.

Fiction & Non-Fiction

Colour Books and Fiction

COLOUR BOOKS

Great new titles for boys and girls from eight to twelve. Fascinating full-colour pictures on every page. Intriguing, authentic, easy-to-read facts.

DINOSAURS   Jane Werner Watson
SECRETS OF THE PAST   Eva Knox Evans
SCIENCE AND US   Bertha Morris Parker
INSIDE THE EARTH   Rose Wyler and
Gerald Ames
EXPLORING OTHER WORLDS
Rose Wyler and Gerald Ames
STORMS   Paul E. Lehr
SNAKES AND OTHER REPTILES
George S. Fichter
AIRBORNE ANIMALS   George S. Fichter
25p each   Fit your pocket – Suit your purse

FICTION
For younger readers

ALBERT AND HENRY
Alison Jezard   20p
ALBERT IN SCOTLAND
Alison Jezard   20p